Cowboy Walking Away

Coming Home to North Dakota Book One

Jessie Gussman

Acknowledgments

Cover art by Julia Gussman

Editing by Heather Hayden

Narration by Jay Dyess

Author Services by CE Author Assistant

Listen to a FREE professionally performed and produced audiobook version of this title on Youtube. Search for "Say With Jay" to browse all available FREE Dyess/Gussman audiobooks.

Contents

Chapter 1

Good Communication and willingness to forgive.
– Mary S. from North Carolina

R ose Baldwin pushed a hair back on her face and wished she were anywhere else.

Anywhere.

Even a snake pit would be better than this.

Laughter cut into her thoughts, and she grabbed the pan of mashed potatoes, taking it to the second table on the right in the church basement in Sweet Water, North Dakota.

The second table on the right was a table that she'd been avoiding as much as she could, all evening.

Since there were only two servers, herself and her sister, for the annual Sweet Water Sweethearts Valentine's Day banquet, she hadn't been able to get out of serving that table even though she truly wanted to.

There were nine other people at the table other than her ex.

One of those people was the woman Harry had left her for, Leah.

Rose set the mashed potatoes down with a smile, at the opposite end of the table from where Harry and Leah were sitting, and grabbed the empty pan.

"I need a refill on my drink," Leah called out before Rose could get away.

Rose's smile felt like her teeth would break, but she nodded and said, "I'll be right back."

"Oh, honey! Take my glass," she called out.

Since Patty's Diner was only catering the event, not hosting it in their restaurant, they weren't bringing new glasses but refilling the old ones.

Rose knew this. She just had a memory lapse, since she worked at Patty's Diner and was used to bringing new glasses with each drink.

"Thank you," she said as she took the glass from Leah, who probably wasn't looking at her in a smug, arrogant kind of way, even though it seemed like she was.

Rose definitely didn't look over at Harry.

Which was quite a feat, since he was sitting so close to Leah, his arm wrapped around her, and Leah was practically pasted to his side.

A person would think after three years of Harry being gone, it wouldn't bother her at all.

The empty potato container in one hand, Leah's glass in the other, Rose strode to the kitchen area where Patty herself was doing dishes in the sink and where the bottles of soda and gallons of water were sitting on the countertop.

"I hope we don't run out of mashed potatoes," Patty said with her back toward Rose. "I don't think we have time to make any more."

"There's a big box of instant mashed potatoes in the cupboard. We could probably use that if we absolutely had to, as long as we replace it," said Lavender, Rose's sister who had volunteered to serve with her, as she brought an empty pan of meatloaf back.

"I hate to do that, because I like to make real mashed potatoes, but you're right. Keep an eye on it and let me know when that pan on the stove is empty."

Lavender glanced at her sister, and Rose said, "We will."

Lavender didn't work at the diner, but when they had needed help to serve the banquet, she'd volunteered, since anyone who had a significant other was at the banquet and help was limited.

Rose took a minute to shove back the hair that had fallen out from underneath the headband she wore along with her ponytail.

Lavender came over, putting her arm around Rose's waist and leaning close to her ear. "The guy's a jerk, and so is she. Don't let them get to you."

"Thanks. He's really not. It's just...this wasn't the way these things were supposed to go." She gave her sister a sidelong glance before she picked up Leah's glass and poured diet soda into it.

"Whether he gets it now, or whether God deals with him in some other way. It's coming. You know that."

"I know. Thanks for reminding me," Rose said as she picked up the glass and walked back out.

Harry had been married to Rose for five years. In that time, Rose had begged to have children, and Harry had put her off, saying he wanted to be more established financially and that they had plenty of time to have kids later.

That was after telling Rose before they were married that he wanted to start a family right away.

It was also before he walked out on Rose and walked into Leah's marriage.

Rose wasn't entirely sure the particulars, since she'd never specifically talked to Harry or Leah about it, but according to Leah's husband Chuck, Leah and Harry were texting long before Leah left. Rose couldn't say for sure Harry had been texting Leah before he walked out on her.

Because she had trusted him, completely, blindly, and, as it turned out, stupidly.

So now, three years later, he acted like he was madly in love with the woman he'd left her for, and they had a happy family of four children, since Leah had three, and they'd immediately had a child of their own as soon as they left their spouses.

While Rose was alone.

She set the glass down in front of Leah and murmured "you're welcome," even though she didn't hear "thank you," and moved to another table where she took an empty plate and a container that needed to be filled up with more bean casserole.

She supposed she didn't have to be alone. She'd been asked out more than once, but...it was just hard to trust anyone after what she'd been through. She really didn't want to, except... Her eyes went to Harry and Leah again. Except they looked so happy together, and that burned her.

That her ex had lied. That he'd cheated, that he'd kept her from having children.

He'd done all of those things, and now he was the one with the big happy family, and she was the one who was alone, even though she was the one who had done right.

God? It's not fair!

She didn't need the Good Lord to remind her that life wasn't fair.

She also didn't need Lavender to remind her that eventually Harry would have to face the Lord where his works would be judged.

She appreciated those reminders though, because sometimes, like now, it was hard not to be bitter.

"Rose!" Charlene called out from beside her sweetheart, Charlie. They were also sitting at the second table on the right.

Rose walked over to the table, reluctantly, unable to turn down a direct request and also unwilling to ignore Charlene, who had been extremely supportive of her and probably knew just as much as her mother did about what had gone on.

Charlene headed up the Sweet Water quilting club and had been instrumental in getting the club to take Rose under their wings for those first few months when she'd been devastated beyond words at Harry's betrayal.

"You look like you're having a great time, Miss Charlene," Rose said, standing so her shoulder was toward Harry and Leah, directly across from Miss Charlene.

"The food is excellent, as always. Miss Patty is a magician in the kitchen," Charlene said, pausing for a moment to wait for Leah's laugh to fade away.

It was probably just Rose's imagination that she had a laugh that could grate on anyone's nerves.

Really, Leah was probably an extremely nice lady. Rose's opinion was biased.

"Can I get you anything?" Rose asked, just wanting to get away. There were eleven other tables, and most of them were packed full. Lavender had been doing a great job of making sure that this table had been taken care of without Rose having to spend much time at it.

"No. Palmer and Ames were just saying that Derek Fields had moved back into town, and I was wondering if you had heard the news. You and he were in the same class in school, weren't you?"

"We were," Rose said, remembering Derek well. And also having heard bits and pieces of the gossip that had been going on in his life.

"His grandparents weren't doing very well," Charlene said, her face showing her concern.

"I was disappointed to hear that. Their spread isn't far from ours, and I think his grandparents were thinking about selling. Now he's back, hopefully to help them and keep the farm from being sold," Palmer said, leaning casually back in his chair, one arm around his wife, Ames, whose rosy cheeks and athletic build suited someone who worked at the Olympic training center that had been built several years ago just outside of Sweet Water. "Although I suppose I would have been interested in buying."

"I don't think we have time for more land anyway, Palmer," Ames said, smiling at her husband, her eyes twinkling. Like she knew exactly what he was going to say.

"A farmer always has time for more ground," he said, and Ames's smile just got bigger, like that was exactly what she had been expecting.

They didn't get out without their four children too much, but they still acted like a young couple in love, not like they were approaching middle age. They must be in their forties since they had both been older than her in school.

"He might not be interested, but he was when he was younger," Charlene said, and Rose nodded, remembering that Derek had wanted to settle down on his grandparents' farm, but he'd ended up moving to The Cities because the girl he was with didn't want to marry a farmer.

"If you're trying to match Rose up, I know for a fact that Derek and Rose would be terrible together. Derek's been living in The Cities for over ten years, and he's very debonair. He might have grown up here in Sweet Water, but he's not a hick anymore. I've actually spoken to him several times, since our parents are good friends." Leah joined the conversation from across the table, and

Rose shifted her body just a little so that she wasn't being completely rude by blocking her out.

Even though she wanted to.

"Rose is quite a catch, and any man would be crazy not to be interested in her," Charlene said, despite the fact that Harry had obviously been not interested in her.

Leah picked up on that right away. "I think that's a false statement. After all, Harry has excellent taste."

"Might be the other way around," Harry muttered, maybe referring to the fact that he thought any man who was interested in Rose would be crazy.

Rose wasn't sure, and she didn't ask for clarification.

Ames and Palmer were whispering at the other end, and Ty and Louise hadn't even looked up from where their heads were bent together. They were taking the whole sweethearts' banquet thing literally. Maybe because they'd spent so much time apart before they'd finally gotten together and gotten married, or maybe that's just the way their relationship was, but they always seemed to be deeply involved with each other. Almost to the point of shutting the world out like they didn't even realize there *was* a world.

Rose wouldn't mind a relationship like that. Where some man wanted her so much that he didn't care about the rest of the world.

He was only interested in her.

It was a nice daydream but probably something that would never happen. She'd have to get past the idea that all men were cheaters.

Even though she knew it wasn't so, she really didn't want to go back down that road. As much as she wanted to be cherished and loved by someone, longed to be, she also did not want to be the laughingstock of everyone ever again in her life.

"It's okay, Rose. After all, we need people to serve the sweethearts' banquet, and you can hardly do that if you're with someone," Harry said, and maybe there was a slight smirk on his face, or maybe that was just Rose's imagination.

"Actually, I am with someone," she said.

She wanted to slap her hand over her mouth. That wasn't the slightest bit true. Why had she said it?

And why wasn't she correcting herself immediately?

But she didn't and allowed herself a bit of a smug look at the astonishment on Harry's and Leah's faces.

Why was she doing this? She was just going to have to confess the truth and be embarrassed.

"Oh? That's interesting," Leah said, rolling her eyes a little, and Rose turned away. Already ashamed of her lie.

Knowing she should just admit that the words had popped out, almost in self-defense, maybe because her heart was just so tired of being painfully beaten up all the time. So it threw those words up and out they came.

Yeah. If only. It just showed a lack of character on her part. That she would prefer to lie rather than graciously accept the truth.

"I heard rumors of you with someone. It's getting pretty serious now?" Charlene said, and Rose managed to not fall on her neck and kiss her, but it was hard.

"It is. He's a great guy. He's so honest. And he doesn't lie." Like those were two separate things. Yeah. She hadn't realized she could be so catty.

"You want a good man with character. Don't settle for anything less," Charlie said from the other side of Charlene. He didn't typically talk much, but when he did, Rose always listened. Usually what he said was wise and laced thoroughly with common sense.

"Yeah. Some of us have learned that the hard way," Rose said, wanting to back away from the table and leave before any of the other couples heard what they were saying and asked her about it. Right now, it was just Leah and Harry, it wouldn't be a big deal.

"What's his name?" Leah asked, of course. Of course she would ask what his name was.

"Would you mind filling up my glass, please?" Charlene said immediately, holding up her mostly full glass of water. "I'm not sure how all the ice melted. I don't like it when it gets to room temperature."

Charlene had specifically requested no ice in her glass when they'd been pouring it earlier.

Grateful for the reprieve, Rose took it immediately. "Of course."

"So there's no name to this mystery boyfriend?" Leah said, like that's exactly what she was expecting.

"Of course not. There is no name, there's no man, and there won't ever be. For reasons that are obvious to everyone," Harry said, and there was no question that he was being a jerk. Rose couldn't even try to find a way to sugarcoat that.

"Oh, there is one all right," Miss Charlene said. "They're all signed up for the Dating Game fun night we're having next month. In fact, they're probably the couple most likely to win." Maybe Miss Charlene's voice was slightly higher than normal, since it seemed to carry over all of their table, and several people at the next table looked over.

As much as Rose wanted to hug Miss Charlene, she also wanted to shake her. How was she going to get out of this lie now? She'd have to have a major breakup with a mystery man she didn't even know the name of.

"Interesting," Leah said, acting like she knew for a fact that everyone around her was lying.

Funny, because they had just been talking about people with character and how honesty was a trait to look for.

Apparently Rose didn't even qualify to date herself.

"I'm definitely looking forward to that. You can sign Harry and me up." Leah smiled at Harry, and they shared a romantic kiss. "I'm sure that true love will win the day, and Harry and I will come out on top," she said, not even trying to be subtle anymore.

Rose held up Miss Charlene's glass. "I'll be back in a minute."

She walked away, wondering how she got herself into these kinds of things.

No. She knew.

She'd spent years and years and years with a lie never crossing her lips, always being honest, always doing right, always choosing the best path, and being kind no matter how unkind people were to her, and then one little slipup, one little white lie, one little defense against people who pounded constantly at her bruised and beaten heart, just once, she did something wrong, and immediately judgment fell.

God? It's really not fair.

She knew by now that there was no point in pointing that out. No matter how true it was, it didn't matter. Life wasn't fair. And someone who was good all their life didn't get credit for that if they chose to lie.

She wanted to keep walking, through the kitchen, out the door, and out into the North Dakota vastness.

To be somewhere, anywhere, other than here.

But they still had the Jell-O salad to serve, and the cake, and she couldn't leave until everything was cleaned up, washed, dried, and put away.

"Are you engaged?" Lavender asked, rushing into the kitchen and going straight for Rose.

At the sink, Patty lifted her head and turned around, her mouth open.

"Yes?" Rose focused on pouring cold water into Charlene's glass. Her word came out as a question, not an answer, but apparently that was enough for Lavender.

"You're engaged!" Lavender squealed. "Why haven't you told anyone?" She grinned. "He asked you on Valentine's Day, didn't he? And...wait!!! Who?!"

"I'm sorry. I know you're excited, and I'm sorry I haven't said anything, but I have to get this water back. We can talk in a little bit."

Normally she would never leave her sister like that, but she had no idea of what to say.

She carried the water back to Charlene's table, and thankfully the entire table was engaged in a rousing discussion of the price of corn, and the weather pattern they'd been in, and everyone had their own prediction for what the weather was going to be this year, so she was able to set the water down and slip away.

She went to the table at the far end, where George and Thelma were sitting with their daughter, Gracie. They were the only ones who had brought a child, and they had been seated at the table with Frank and Jean, the only couple who had brought their dog, Blondie.

Technically, neither kids nor dogs were supposed to be at the banquet, since it was a sweethearts' banquet, but no one made anyone strictly adhere to the rules, and if they couldn't find a sitter or didn't want to leave their dog at home, it wasn't a big deal.

It was Sweet Water after all, and people rolled with things.

So far Gracie and Blondie had been eyeing each other, and it seemed like Gracie wanted to pet the dog, but Blondie didn't seem too interested in children, ignoring people in general.

"Blondie's home all the time so we had to bring her, because she needs to be socialized. We want to get her certified to be an elderly companion, and in order to do that, Blondie needs to be socialized while she's young with lots of people," Jean had explained to Rose when she'd first gone over to serve them, although Rose hadn't asked and certainly didn't care if the dog was at the sweethearts' banquet.

Blondie lay beside Jean, her ears flattening against her head every time Gracie looked at her.

She was young, and if Rose was any judge of dogs, she was terrified as well.

The other people at the table had been fine as well, and the dog had helped guide them into conversations that involved all the dogs everyone had ever owned with one old-timer telling a story about a blue heeler he used to have and how it went out every night and guarded their home, and with the way the man was embellishing the tale, Rose figured by the time he was done the dog would be making supper and doing rounds in the hospital as well.

Obviously, the guy had been fond of his dog.

Seeing that they were ready for the Jell-O salad, she walked back to the kitchen and grabbed a pan along with some new dessert plates.

"You are awful!" Lavender said as she hurried past, food in one hand and two glasses in the other, and Rose wanted nothing more than to tell her that it was all a big farce. Lavender would understand, even agree. And she'd probably keep up the pretense tonight and help her figure out a way to get out of it.

But she didn't want her sister to have to lie for her. Plus, people were finishing up their meals, and they needed to clear the tables, get dessert plates out, and set out the Jell-O salad and the cake.

"I'll tell you all about it later," Rose said, wishing she didn't have to say anything at all.

"Hey! Is that ours? That looks great!" a man said as she walked by his table with the Jell-O salad in one hand and the dessert plates in the other.

Noticing that his table was ready too, she set the Jell-O salad down along with the plates.

It was another ten minutes before she made it back to the back table with the child and the dog.

By that time, Gracie had gotten bored with no food in front of her and was off her chair, glancing at her parents and obviously trying to move around without them noticing.

She'd probably been told to sit still, but her desire to pet the dog overcame her desire to do what her parents wanted her to.

Rose smiled. She remembered being a child and wanting a dog more than anything. A dog of her own, something to cuddle up with at night, something to go places with, and something that loved her no matter what.

She supposed every child probably went through a stage where they wanted a pet.

Maybe after tonight, George and Thelma would consider doing that for Gracie, since she was an only child and probably lonely.

Setting the Jell-O salad down, she grabbed empty plates so she could pass out the dessert plates, and they'd be ready for cake.

Concentrating on her task, she barely registered that someone at the table had just said that German shepherds make better cattle dogs than blue heelers, which caused something close to a heated argument at the table, when growling and barking and a squeal interrupted everything.

Gracie had managed to move away from her chair and over to Blondie. Blondie must have backed away from her until the dog was cowering against the wall.

By the looks of things, Gracie had figured she would be able to catch Blondie and possibly pick her up, although Rose couldn't be sure. Whatever happened, the dog had been frightened enough to snap at the little girl. Gracie squealed while the dog growled and bit her face.

Rose didn't think twice but yelled, waving her arms and running toward the dog.

Her family owned an auction house, and she dealt with animals on a weekly basis. She helped every Wednesday and Saturday at the auction along with her job at the diner.

They'd never run a dog through the auction barn, but in her experience, any animal could be intimidated if a person looked big and scary enough.

It was also her experience that there were times where it was beneficial to try to calm a scared animal down, to soothe them with pretty words and slow movements.

But when an animal was attacking, especially when a child was involved, it was faster and safer to be big and scary, at least until everyone had been moved out of the danger area and into a safe place.

It was just natural instinct for Rose to do what she did, since it's what she would have done at the auction barn. Sure enough, the dog backed up, and she was able to angle herself, coming in from the side and chasing the dog away from the crying little girl.

Figuring that the dog wasn't coming back—she had only snapped because she was scared of the little creature—Rose knelt down.

Gracie's face was bleeding, and Gracie was sobbing and scared, calling for her mom.

The dog's teeth had yanked down on Gracie's cheek, and there would be a scar, surely, but the wounds weren't fatal.

Thelma took one look and started hyperventilating, fanning herself, looking petrified and anxious.

Rose glanced up, one hand holding the little girl's hand, one hand stroking her head.

"Settle," she said sharply, and Thelma's eyes focused on her. "Look," she said, shifting her voice to a soft, calming tone, hoping that Thelma could hear her over Gracie's sobs. "You need to calm down so Gracie sees you're not scared. She'll be brave if you are."

She didn't have children of her own, but she had babysat a lot of kids through high school. Her whole dream in life had been to be a wife and mother. She knew that wasn't what women were expected to do in the modern world, and it wasn't something that she told a lot of people, but when she got married, it was the one thing she wanted: children.

So maybe she didn't know them like a mother might, but she did have a good bit of knowledge, and she knew it to be true. Children had a tendency to mirror the emotions of the adults they were with.

Whether it was her words, or whether it was Thelma finally coming to her senses, Rose didn't know, but she straightened her face, drew in a breath, and knelt down on the other side of her daughter.

George stepped in, and Rose stood up and backed away so they could kneel on either side of their child.

Her heart hurt, because she was sure the parents were upset with themselves and scared.

Looking up, she could see that Frank and Jean had grabbed a hold of Blondie and had her calmed down. It looked like they were taking her out, and Rose figured that was probably for the best.

Everything seemed to be taken care of, so she went to the kitchen, washed her hands, and went back out to do her job. She felt terrible for not just Gracie, but for her parents, and also for Blondie. Hopefully they'd understand that the dog wasn't a terrible dog, just wasn't ready to be handled by small children.

Regardless, she was grateful that the talk for the rest of the evening was about the dog, the attack, and debate on whose fault it was, along with stories people told about being attacked by dogs or witnessing dog attacks, and everyone seemed to forget that Rose had suddenly become engaged. For the evening anyway.

Chapter 2

Trust and communication are 2 big factors.
- Tonya Schultz from Southern California

Derek Fields walked in from the barn, carrying the eggs he'd gathered while he'd been feeding the orphan calves that they kept in the corral close to the barnyard.

He'd forgotten how much he loved this life.

When Stephanie had made him move to The Cities in order to be with her, he'd hated giving it up, but eventually life had gone on, and he forgot.

He wasn't sure that he would say coming back had been the best decision he'd ever made, but he wouldn't be surprised if eventually he felt that way.

Grateful that the man his grandparents had hired to oversee the farm had quit, he realized he probably wouldn't be back here if they had been able to hire someone.

It seemed like there was a shortage of employees everywhere, and people who were getting hired expected to be compensated at least twice as much as what his grandparents were expecting to pay or could afford.

He had firsthand experience with this with his corporate job and also because he'd been trying to hire a companion for his grandparents for several months now. Since he'd been home at Christmastime and had seen how they struggled at times.

They weren't incapable of taking care of themselves, but he would feel better if there was someone there to do hard things, like carry laundry upstairs and bring things up from the cellar.

It hadn't been a hard decision to leave his corporate job and come back to Sweet Water.

After all, Stephanie had just left him six months ago, and he loved the excuse to get out of the city.

"Good morning," he said as he walked into the big farm kitchen, shaking the snow off his boots and switching the eggs from one hand to the other as he shrugged out of his heavy winter jacket.

North Dakota felt colder than Minnesota. Whether it actually was or not, he wasn't entirely sure, but North Dakota was wilder. More open. Less civilized. Maybe that was the difference.

He liked the wildness though. It made him feel like he'd been a city boy for too long.

His grandparents looked up from the table, and Gram smiled, putting her hands down and pushing back from her chair as she said, "Good morning. Looks like you found us breakfast," as she reached for the eggs he carried.

"Only five today. It's pretty cold out."

"They don't usually lay when it gets below zero. Actually, they quit before that. You can almost tell the weather by them," Pap said, leaning back in his chair and looking at his grandson like he was the best thing that had happened to him in a long time.

Maybe it was. His kids hadn't been interested in the farm, none of them, and were now scattered over the United States.

North Dakota could be brutal; not everyone stayed.

Derek had always loved it. He'd only left because he thought he found something he loved more. Someone.

Maybe he had, but she hadn't loved him.

Or had fallen out of love, or whatever it was that people did when they thought it was okay to leave their marriage and hook up with someone else.

"Get yourself a cup of coffee and get some warmth in you, and I'll have breakfast cooked up in no time. I already have the bacon on the stove."

"I can smell it. I think that's why I probably came in from the barn early."

"I thought you were in kinda quick," Pap said with a grin.

Derek had only been back a week, but he felt settled in and like he'd been back for a lot longer.

"Miss Charlene said that some little girl was bitten by a dog last night at the sweethearts' banquet," his grandma said, making conversation as she cracked the eggs into a bowl.

"A dog? A kid? At the sweethearts' banquet. When did that change from couples to kids and dogs?" he asked, pouring steaming coffee into his mug.

Gram laughed. "It hasn't changed that much. You know there's always a couple or two who feel like they need to bring something. I guess George and Thelma didn't want to leave little Gracie at home. She doesn't do well with the babysitter and cries the whole time. And Frank and Jean were trying to socialize their dog."

"At a Valentine's sweethearts' banquet? That's a good idea," Derek said, just a little sarcastically. Why would someone bring their dog to a sweethearts' banquet?

Thinking of dogs, he kind of thought maybe they should get one. They'd always had one around the farm when he'd been growing up, so he asked, "Why don't you have a dog?"

The kitchen was silent for a moment, almost as though Gram was waiting for Pap to answer, and Pap was waiting for Gram to answer.

Finally Gram said, "Well, Derek. We're getting older, and if we get a dog, there's a good chance we might be dead before he is."

"Dead or have to sell the farm. One of the two. Either one doesn't seem very fair to the dog."

Derek hadn't considered that, and he stared at his grandparents.

Sure, they were in their seventies, but that wasn't terribly old. Neither one of them acted like they were old, exactly. Although he had been searching for a helper for them, it wasn't necessarily because they were old, just because...they weren't getting around as well as they used to.

Which kind of meant they were getting old.

Funny how he didn't want to see the things that were right in front of his face.

Like his wife texting another man and him never noticing.

"Well, I'm back now, and I'm planning on staying. At least for the lifetime of a dog. Maybe that's something we can think about." It reminded him that he needed to work something out with his grandparents.

He wasn't exactly sure where the lines were. He'd told Gram and Pap he would buy the farm from them, but they said that they wanted to think about it. Something about not wanting him to have to pay for all of it, if he was going to work there, and he supposed it was a big step.

It kind of left him in limbo though. Not exactly sure where he stood.

It was one of those conversations that could end up being awkward but that he knew they'd need to have eventually.

He pulled out a chair and sat down at the table, setting his coffee in front of him after taking a tentative sip.

It was hot and burned his tongue, but it warmed him all the way to his stomach.

"I'm fine with that." Pap leaned forward, looking thoughtful. "Are you sure you want to stay? Because your grandma and I have been talking about it and would really like to see that. Like to see the farm stay in the family. And we'd like to try to make that happen if you're sure."

"I am. I know North Dakota isn't for everyone. But..." He didn't want to say he wouldn't have left if it hadn't been for Stephanie, but for some reason, that made him feel weak. Like he'd been a fool to give up something that was solid and unchanging for a woman. One who turned his world upside down, led him around like a puppy on a string, and then kicked him to the curb.

Yeah, his experience with Stephanie had made him feel like less than a man.

He wouldn't even have said that was possible, but it was true.

North Dakota would be able to heal that hole in his heart, he was almost sure of it.

Maybe that was why God had made places like this. Places where man could still pit himself against nature, and come out the winner, and feel better for it. Maybe God knew a man needed that fight, that struggle, that victory.

Or maybe it was just him.

"I need to talk to your grandma a little bit, but maybe we can plan on talking about that this weekend, and we'll come up with something. In the meantime, if you see a dog, by all means, a rancher should have a dog by his side."

"Your grandpa and I always did. I'm sure you remember them over the years."

"I remember three. Just one at a time, and they always followed Pap around, coming into the house and lying down in front of the front door. They didn't go any farther."

"No. They always knew their place was at the front door, until the last one. Somehow, I guess we got soft or something in our old age, and before we knew it, she was in the living room, and then she was upstairs, in our bed."

"Don't let your grandma fool you. She loved that dog, and I'm pretty sure she loved her more than me, because she slipped between us."

Derek snorted, glad he hadn't put his coffee to his lips yet. That was more than he'd known about Sadie, their last dog.

He'd known Gram had loved her.

"I can't believe you let something come between you and Gram," he teased Pap.

"I didn't have a choice. Your grandma told me if I didn't like Sadie between us, I could go sleep on the couch. I figured if I put up too much of a fuss, she'd have me sleeping in front of the front door."

They laughed, and Gram soon had breakfast ready. They ate before he checked the weather on his phone and announced that he was driving to town.

In small towns, sometimes the best way to get word around was to spread it among the townspeople themselves.

On Sunday, he'd let it be known that he was looking for a helper, and he figured he'd run to the hardware store, grab a few things he needed, and see if anyone had heard of anyone who would be available.

"You guys are welcome to come if you want."

"No. It's pretty cold out today, and we were just in town on Sunday."

It truly was cold—with the wind chills, it was well below zero—but there wasn't much snow on the ground, and the roads would be good. But he understood. He supposed when he got older, it would be nicer to stay inside in the warm house than to brave the cold North Dakota wind.

Especially in February, after a person had put up with three or four months of winter already.

He drove to town, stopping at the hardware store and picking up what he needed, casually asking if anyone had heard of anyone who was looking for a job. Hoping for a woman. He couldn't imagine a man wanting to hang out with his grandparents, although he didn't want to close himself off to the possibilities. A man could be just as good of a caretaker as a woman, and if someone needed a job, it might be something they would be interested in.

Plus, Gram seemed to be taking things in stride but would probably be the one to be the most upset about selling the farm. Having a woman around she could talk to might be a good idea.

Still, he was assured that no one had heard anything, so he strolled down to the diner, thinking he might grab a piece of pie and catch up on the latest since that was really the heart of the town.

Wind blasted down the street, and he shrugged down in his coat, waiting until the wind died down a bit before he opened the door.

Sometimes the wind would catch it and throw it back against the wall. He didn't want to break any glass this morning. That might hurt business.

It was late enough that the breakfast rush had diminished, and he was actually the only patron in the dining area.

Although Miss Patty was talking to someone—a waitress with an apron tied around her waist, but he couldn't see her face since she stood with her back mostly toward him.

He didn't want to interrupt them, so he walked to a table and sat down, picking up the menu that was on it and scanning the list of pies. Might as well be ready to order when Patty came out so he could ask about whether she knew of someone who was looking for a job.

Normally there was music playing or something piping from the speakers, but there wasn't today, and he realized as he scanned the menu that he could hear the conversation clearly.

He didn't mean to listen, but it was impossible not to hear what they were saying.

"I'm sorry. You know that I wouldn't do this if I had any choice, but Denise's family, and my sister, will kill me if I don't give her a job. And...it's winter."

"I understand. It's a slow time, and you can't afford to have both of us." The other lady, whose voice he didn't recognize, sounded resigned.

"I knew you'd understand, and I appreciate that." Miss Patty sounded relieved, though her expression held more than a little regret. "Honestly, Denise has never stuck with one thing very long, and I'm sure she won't be here more than a few weeks, a month at the most. I hate displacing a longtime employee especially with someone that I can't even depend on, but...family."

"I understand completely. Sometimes there are just things you have to do in order to keep the peace and make holidays bearable."

"Exactly. My parents would never understand if I didn't hire my niece, especially when she's down and out."

Funny, because Derek had firsthand experience, knowing that there were jobs open everywhere. The niece shouldn't have a problem getting a job and shouldn't need to displace a valued employee, unless of course Denise had a record of not being dependable and couldn't come up with references who would give her a good recommendation.

Derek kept his mouth shut though, because he knew how things went in the business world. People who deserved promotions often didn't get them, and people who didn't have a clue what they were doing were often promoted well beyond their capabilities, just because they knew someone or were related to someone.

He'd been passed over more than once because of that.

It was just the way the world was.

Still, he squirmed to be overhearing the conversation and was grateful when the woman sighed and said, "I get it. I can grab my things. They're in the back."

She wore sneakers, and he didn't hear her walk away, but Miss Patty's flip-flops signaled her arrival at his table.

"I'm sorry. I didn't hear you come in. I hope you haven't been waiting long."

"No." He didn't mention that he'd been sitting there long enough to hear her can someone. "Just long enough to peruse the pies selection and know that there's about seven different kinds that I'd like to have."

"I can get you a piece of each," Miss Patty said, her smile friendly, even if there was a lingering tightness to her eyes that said she really regretted what she'd had to do.

Then a thought occurred to him. Whoever she just fired would be looking for a job.

Could he ask about her?

She didn't know he overheard the conversation, which wasn't exactly his fault, but he thought of employee regulations and figured that even if Miss Patty would tell him, she probably shouldn't.

Man, he still wanted to, just because that would be almost perfect. And he could get a recommendation right here. All he had to do was ask Miss Patty if the lady that she just fired was trustworthy. But she must have been since Miss Patty obviously didn't want to let her go.

Regardless, he ordered his pie, ate it, and chatted with Miss Patty as she cleaned the one dirty table in a leisurely manner, waiting for the best time to ask and not make it seem like he'd overheard, because he still wanted to see if there was anybody she would recommend who was looking for a job.

Turned out, he didn't even have to ask.

"You know, I just remembered you were in here last week asking if I knew of anyone who was looking for a job. You were, right?"

"I was," he said, between mouthfuls.

"You're looking for someone to take care of your grandparents? Or not take care of them, you just wanted...like a helper for odds and ends and stuff?"

"Yeah. Just someone to carry laundry, maybe do some house-cleaning to take a little of the burden off Gram, run up and down the steps so they don't have to. Maybe clean the bathtub so they don't have to get down. That type of thing. Maybe this spring, they could help out in the garden." He was just kind of going through his mind, trying to think of the things that Gram always did that maybe she wasn't able to do as well anymore.

"I wish you could have come in a little earlier, because Rose Baldwin might be interested." She leaned closer to him and lowered her voice, even though he was still the only person in the dining area. "I had to fire her this morning, because my niece Denise needs a job. She's supposed to be here..." She looked at her watch. "She was supposed to be here ten minutes ago. And that's why I didn't want to let Rose go. She is an excellent worker and has been here for years, but...my sister will make my life extremely difficult if I don't hire my niece, and I can't afford to keep them both. Not in February in North Dakota."

"I get it." Just like Rose, he understood. And now he had a name to go with the back of the head that he'd seen.

He remembered her from school, although they had never really hung out. Still, she was a local girl, and her family was well respect-ed. They owned the auction barn outside of Sweet Water. He felt less bad for her being fired because he knew she would have a job there.

Still, she would be perfect for his gram.

"I remember her," he said. "Did she say she would be interested in some other position?"

"No. But she's always supplemented her income at the auction barn by working here. She really seems to like it. I don't know if it's the people or just having something outside of the family business. Some people are like that," Miss Patty said.

"You have her contact info?" he asked.

"I don't think I can give that out, employee privacy and all, but she was headed over to the church basement for the quilting meeting. You might be able to catch her there if you hurry," Miss Patty said. "Not that I'm running you off, because I'll gladly get you another piece of pie."

"No thank you. That piece of cherry was delicious, but it was enough."

He could have just walked in and asked and not had pie. Probably that would have been better for his health, but he didn't regret it. The pie was delicious, and he had a name. He considered the trip worthwhile.

He paid his bill, getting three pieces of pie to go, figuring it would be dessert for supper tonight with his grandparents, and headed out. He'd run into the church before heading home.

He put the pie in his truck and jogged across the street, turning down along the church and going to the basement door, stopping with his hand on the doorknob.

As he recalled, these meetings could get quite rowdy, having attended a few with his grandma over the years back when he was younger. Maybe the ladies had gotten more sedate as they got older, but somehow he kind of doubted it.

Steeling himself, he twisted the knob and walked in.

Chapter 3

Remembering to laugh and forgive and pray!
- Betty Mackintosh from South Carolina

R ose shoved her hands deep into the pockets of her coat and ducked down against the wind, walking behind the church and stepping into the basement.

She didn't always go to the quilting meetings, and she hadn't been planning on attending this one, but since she was now jobless, she figured she might as well.

Wherever she went, she was going to face questions. If she showed up at home before they were expecting her, they were going to want to know what happened, and she really didn't want to have to talk about her being fired.

She'd never been let go from a position in her life before, and she had to admit it stunk.

Even though she knew it wasn't because of something that she had done wrong, that there wasn't any problem on her part, it still hurt.

Like a rejection: *You are not good enough.*

She tried to get her mind off that, because it made her chin tremble, and she wanted to cry.

Not that crying would solve anything. It's just how she felt.

Everyone looked up when she stepped in, and she realized belatedly that maybe this was a bad choice too.

She should have just gone to the library. Buried her nose in a book for a bit, until she felt she could face everyone at home.

These ladies weren't going to ask why she was off her job early, but they were going to ask what she was going to do about the almost-fiancé that she didn't have.

Or if they didn't ask, at least they would remind her that she needed to do something about that.

Things had been too crazy with the dog biting Gracie, and she hadn't wanted to walk over to Harry and Leah's table and just announce that she'd lied.

Even though she had, and that's what she should have done. Then she wouldn't be facing this double whammy this morning. Being fired and still needing to admit to her cheating ex-husband and his marriage-wrecking wife that she'd lied.

"Rose!" Charlene said, standing and holding her hands out. Pieces of material lay scattered all over the table in front of her. "It's been so cold, only Vicki and Kathy could make it. We're glad to see you!" Charlene said, coming forward and hugging her, and Rose had no doubt that her words were true. Charlene truly was happy to see her.

She felt like she could melt into the maternal hug. She hadn't realized how much she'd needed that solace.

"What happened?" Charlene said, seeming to know instinctively that something was wrong. Because Rose hadn't said anything. She wasn't even crying.

Or hadn't been.

Her eyes filled. "Miss Patty's niece is coming to the diner, and she had to let me go."

"Oh, that's terrible!" Vicki said, standing and coming over. "I'm so sorry to hear it!"

She wrapped her arms around Rose as well, and name came over also, clucking like a hen who was worried about her chick.

The three of them just stood there with their arms around Rose, and that was all she needed.

Not someone to tell her what she needed to do, or to tell her that it wasn't her fault, which she already knew, or that Denise would probably be gone in a month, or whatever. It didn't matter. They just hugged her and made her feel loved, and she didn't want to ever leave the shelter of their arms.

But eventually they pulled back.

"It doesn't matter what the reasons are, it's never easy to have someone tell you you're not wanted anymore," Charlene said, her arm wrapped around Rose as they walked toward the table where the quilting pieces were spread out.

"I know. I just...the last couple of days have been such a disaster."

She looked around, unsure whether Charlene had told Vicki and Kathy about her made-up fiancé.

"They know. But we decided that only the people that came to the quilting meeting today were going to find out. So this is all the further it's going."

The ladies were not exactly known as gossips around Sweet Water, but they did have a tendency to move information. Usually not in a vindictive or unkind way, though.

Which is what Rose had always associated with gossips.

Still, Rose also knew that if the ladies had decided not to say anything, nothing would get them to open their mouths. They were as trustworthy and loyal as people could be.

She breathed a sigh of relief as she settled down in her chair. "I don't know what to do about that either."

She didn't really mean that she didn't know what to do. She did. What she needed to do was admit the truth. That there was no one else. There was no man. No significant other. No engagement.

Nothing.

"I've actually been thinking about that, and I have an idea," Charlene said, her fingers moving over the quilt pieces as she spoke, as though quilting came automatically, and it was something she could do without thinking. Which was probably true.

"What's that?" Rose asked warily. Tired. Knowing that whatever the idea was, it was going to involve her in a very uncomfortable and unwanted situation.

She wished there was a way she could put it off without making it bigger. But the sooner she did it, the less embarrassed she'd be.

"I was thinking we could hire someone to be your fake boyfriend," Charlene said, like that was the most natural thing in the world. Hiring a boyfriend.

"You want me to hire a boyfriend?" She couldn't keep the sarcasm out of her voice. Was this supposed to make her feel better? She had to make someone up to make herself look better in front of her ex and his loving wife, then she got fired from her job, and now she had to hire someone to like her because no one possibly could without money involved?

She knew she was exaggerating her problems, but they felt bigger than what she could handle right now, and she felt overwhelmed and incredibly unwanted.

Her stomach twisted and her throat closed and she just wanted to find someplace where she could curl into a ball and cry. Maybe for days.

"It's a thought. Listen, I don't like to say these kinds of things, because I don't want to see anyone's marriage not make it. Even someone who had left their first marriage and broke up another one. Even that marriage. I'd like to see it be strong, like to see it work. Most definitely when there are kids involved, but..." Charlene said this, her hand closing over top of Rose's on the table, her head leaning close in, trying to catch Rose's eye. "But watching them last night, there is a huge chasm in their relationship, and they were covering it with scotch tape and plastic. They were acting happy, but there was a lot of tension between them."

Rose knew those words should make her happy, and maybe on one level, a very fleshly, very shallow, very childish level, they did.

But she was like Miss Charlene, she didn't want to see anyone's marriage fail. She just couldn't stand how Harry and Leah seemed to rub in her face that her husband had left her, and now he was happily married to the woman he cheated on her with, and they had lots of children and everything that Rose had ever wanted, and he didn't need her, didn't regret leaving her, and it made her feel like a loser.

"Just hire a boyfriend for a few months. Six months. Make an offer. In fact, the ladies and I've been talking, and we'll take some of the quilting money to help pay for it if you can't."

"I can pay for my own boyfriend!" Rose said, her voice raised despite herself. Then she froze.

Wait. What?

"No! I'm not paying for a boyfriend. No one is paying for a boyfriend for me."

Goodness. If that got out, and in small towns, stuff *always* got out, she would be even more of a laughingstock than just making a boyfriend up. But paying for one? Outrageous.

"Just think about it. Don't shut your mind off to the possibilities before you've considered everything," Vicki said earnestly.

Rose tilted her head. Had these ladies gone mad? They were wanting her to consider hiring a boyfriend? That was crazy.

But she knew that sometimes she truly did come into something with her own bias, like not liking Leah because she broke up her marriage, yanked her kids away from her family, and didn't have a problem carrying on with a married man, who happened to be Rose's husband, and so yeah, she had a bias.

Leah was probably a very nice lady; her friends loved her, and her family couldn't live without her.

So, she stared at Vicki but didn't really see her, trying to roll that problem over in her head. In what galaxy was it a good idea to hire a boyfriend?

Not in this one, came the answer.

That's exactly what she thought.

But apparently her silence encouraged the ladies and gave them hope, because Charlene's hand squeezed over top of hers, and she said, "That's it. Think about it."

"Where is she going to get a boyfriend for hire?" Vicki whispered.

There was some shushing going on, and then Charlene said, "Maybe God will provide him for her."

There was silence in the basement.

The door opened.

Derek Fields stepped in.

The ladies gasped, and one of them whispered, "God provides."

"God provides a lamb," Rose muttered, thinking of Abraham and Isaac and the lamb that got sacrificed in Isaac's place.

Poor Derek had no idea what he was stepping into.

Not to mention, he had been sitting at the table in the diner when Miss Patty had fired her. Talk about embarrassing.

Rose glanced over her shoulder once more, then back to the ladies. Was it too late to duck underneath the table?

The temptation was almost more than she could stand, but she figured she needed some practice in overcoming temptation, since she'd let temptation loosen her tongue and shake a lie out of her normally nothing-but-truthful mouth.

"Derek Fields! I heard that you were back in town." Charlene spoke just as coolly as if they'd been talking about the weather before he stepped in.

"I was in church on Sunday morning, and I was looking for you, Miss Vicki. Where were you?"

"I was out visiting my son. We had a family get-together, and all the boys were home."

"I see. Well, I'm here, in the flesh."

"I heard you're back to stay?" Charlene asked, never one to beat around the bush when a direct question would do.

Rose was glad she asked because she was kind of curious herself. From what she'd heard, Derek had gone through something similar to what she had.

"I am. I've offered to buy the farm from my grandparents, and they're thinking about it. In the meantime, Bud has moved on to Montana, and I'm working on the farm."

"You didn't like your city job?" Kathy said.

"I didn't realize how much I disliked it until I was back here," Derek said, and his words held a ring of honesty and also maybe one of relief. That the stress that he'd had from living in the city had evaporated when he'd come back home.

"I saw you in church on Sunday, Rose, but I didn't get to say anything to you. Good to see you." Derek spoke casually, and it wasn't his fault his benign words made her stomach jump and quiver like she'd just hatched a donkey in it.

"Good to see you. Glad to hear you're sticking around." Rose kept her fingers from gripping together like she was on a roller coaster about to go off the rails.

"Your family still owns the auction house? Livestock exchange?"

"We sure do." She was surprised how calm her voice sounded, considering all of the chaos in her life, which was reflected in her chest feeling like the inside of a ping-pong machine.

All the trouble in her life had seemed to get worse since Derek had walked in, but probably because he was one more person that had witnessed her recent humiliations.

"Funny you should mention that," Charlene said. "Because Rose was just telling us that she was interested in hiring a man, and then you walked in. It seemed like divine intervention."

Rose wasn't sure what that had to do with anything they had been talking about, but sometimes when a person was old, they could get away with things that a normal person couldn't, and Miss Charlene seemed to know that, even though she wasn't terribly old, because Derek just nodded, like what she had said had made perfect sense.

Hopefully, he wasn't nodding because he thought that he was a part of some kind of divine intervention.

Rose had had enough of arrogant men to last for a lifetime. And Derek hadn't been like that in school.

Of course, sometimes people went to the city, and they changed. Not necessarily for the better.

It had ruined more than one person, in her eyes, but again, she understood there was a second view.

"Well, I hope you find the right man for the job," Derek said, taking a break to say something else.

"That's you," Charlene said, like Derek wasn't trying to deflect the attention.

"Back on the farm—"

"Oh, that work won't matter. This job won't take any time away from the farm. Or not much."

"I think I'll have my hands fu—"

"Hear her out before you make up your mind," Miss Vicki said.

Rose decided that hiding under the table wouldn't be good enough. She needed to get a shovel and start digging. Probably she just might as well go to the graveyard and make herself at home. There wasn't much chance of her getting out of this without being completely and totally embarrassed.

Of course, maybe she could take the bull by the horns.

She stood up and faced Derek directly.

Opening her mouth to speak, she realized with a start that he was taller than she remembered. The stubble on his face made him seem a little rugged, and she didn't recall that he had worn a cowboy hat in high school. But it looked good on him now.

A sheepskin jacket completed the cowboy look, and although he wore work boots instead of cowboy boots, his jeans were well-worn even if he had just come back to the farm.

Forcing her mouth to move, remembering that she was going to take charge, she only paused for a second before she said, "I'm sorry. I put my foot in my mouth yesterday. No. That's not true. I lied yesterday. I don't know why. Because I usually don't. In fact, I can't remember the last time I lied."

"You had a reason."

"A lie is a lie." She looked down at Miss Charlene. She couldn't excuse her sin. She had to own it. "Anyway. The ladies are trying to help me out of it, but I think the best thing I can do is just face it. It's going to be embarrassing, and it's probably going to hurt some too, but just forget it. They don't mean anything."

"Oh, we do mean something. And if you're not going to tell him, I will." Miss Vicki stood up, her hands on the table, her eyes narrowed like she truly meant business.

Rose did a double take, because usually Miss Vicki was a very laid-back, sweet lady, but she had raised six boys, so there had to be a backbone there, and it looked like Rose was seeing it.

She didn't want to be talked about like she wasn't here, so she said, "I told my ex that I was involved with someone, because I couldn't stand seeing him and the woman he cheated on me with snuggling up at the table last night at the sweethearts' banquet. I didn't get a chance to say that it wasn't true, that I was...lying... After Grace got bitten by the dog, it kinda flew out of everyone's head. The ladies think it would be a good idea for me to actually hire a boyfriend and make it true. Or seem true anyway. But I can't see doing that. It's just... Who would do that with me anyway? I mean, where am I going to find someone to hire? And I don't even want to do it anyway!" She put her hands on her hips and glared at the ladies, like somehow they were bewitching her, and she was starting to think that hiring someone actually was a good idea.

As she'd spoken, Derek's face had gone from amused interest, to surprise, and back to amused interest, maybe mixed with a little bit of pity.

"You know, I've heard that your husband did that to you. Kinda what my wife did to me. Almost the exact same thing. Maybe slightly different circumstances, but she's now living with a man who has three kids, when she didn't want to have any with me. And I had seen her texting him before she left, and it didn't even occur to me that it might be something that might break up our marriage. I trusted her."

He seemed pained to admit all of that, and Rose could totally understand. She felt the same way.

"But I guess I haven't gotten to the point where I'm so desperate I'd hire a girlfriend. Although…" He tilted his head. "I suppose if I had to see her in town every day or sidled up with some dude who didn't think twice about stepping into somebody else's marriage, I guess… I guess that idea might not seem so unreasonable."

"See!" Charlene jumped on that immediately. "I told you. This isn't such a crazy idea. He just said that he would do the exact same thing!"

"I actually said—"

Miss Charlene gave him a look that made his mouth snap shut. Rose could hear the clack of his teeth from where she stood.

"Listen, Rose," Kathy said, in a gentler, more compassionate voice than anyone had been using. "I know you feel rejected. Maybe like you're unwanted, even a loser."

"Thanks," Rose said.

"But!" Kathy said emphatically. "But the entire town feels for you. There isn't a single person in town that would take Harry's side over you. We all want to see something good happen for you. Lots of good things. We know you were dealt a bad hand. We know you were treated wrong, we know that you're hurt, and we all hurt with you."

Derek shifted, like Kathy's speech was making him uncomfortable, but no one interrupted her.

"Maybe. Maybe we're butting in right now because we really, really want to see Harry get a little bit of what he deserves. You know, you're not the only one who wants that."

Rose raised her eyes. She didn't know what was in Kathy's past. Maybe she was talking about herself. Maybe she was talking about one of her children. Rose wasn't sure, but the thought was plain. Rose hadn't been the only one who had been cheated on, and everyone could understand wanting to see Harry, if not hurt, at least get a little of his own medicine. To reap what he sowed.

"That's for the Lord to hand out. Not me," she said. As badly as she wanted to do it, God had been clear about where vengeance lay, and it wasn't with her.

"Could you do it at least until the Dating Game get-together? You and your significant other are supposed to be there and be playing. And it would be really sweet to see you and him beat Harry and Leah. Please? Beating them would be doing a favor for the whole town."

With the way Charlene was speaking, it was hard for Rose to think of her objections. She knew they were there, right on the tip of her consciousness, but when Charlene made it seem like she would be doing the whole town a favor, when she said that they were all on her side, when she made it seem like they were a team that was pulling together, she didn't want to deny her.

She wanted to do it.

"You pretty much have me talked into it. What exactly are you thinking?" Derek's deep voice came from off to the side. Rose had almost forgotten about him as she had gotten swept up in Charlene's plans and pleading.

Charlene smiled—a satisfied smile—without arrogance. "Rose? Do it for us."

"Derek? Would you be interested in being my fake boyfriend for the next month? We're very close to marriage and seeing each other exclusively." Rose's shoulders slumped. "At least that's what I told him last night."

"I see."

She waited, thinking that no man in his right mind would accept that proposal.

"Yes," Derek said simply. "Or should I demand that you get down on one knee and ask me?"

The ladies tittered, and Rose lifted her head, meeting Derek's eyes and seeing the humor in them.

Okay. If he was going to be funny, if he was going to make her laugh, yeah. Maybe she would enjoy it.

"This is terrible, but maybe there's a little part of me that wouldn't mind seeing your ex get a little bit of what I feel like *my* ex deserves. Not that I want to be mean or vindictive, but I'm okay with playing a little game for a month, no payment necessary. Nothing serious. I don't want to take you home to meet my parents or anything, although... Actually, I'm looking for someone to watch my grandparents, and I don't think I said yes just because of that—" He interrupted himself, and Rose smiled.

Like they were really in a relationship, and she thought he was trying to manipulate her.

"No. Go on."

"Well, I know that you just lost your job. I guess you saw me sitting there."

"I did."

"And I was actually here because Miss Patty said you'd probably be here, and she wouldn't give me your contact info, employment laws and all that, and I wanted to know if you might be interested in watching my grandparents."

"I could do that in exchange for you pretending to be my boyfriend."

"No. I'll pay you for it. I'm not asking for an exchange."

"I was going to pay you for the boyfriend thing."

"I...I told you that I'll do the boyfriend thing without payment. Just because...just because sometimes I think it's okay to play a game, even if it lasts for a month."

"Are we going to look at it like a game, instead of like we're lying?"

"We're pretending. We're pretending for a little bit, maybe the way you would if you were playing a board game or acting in a play. Don't we consider that okay? To pretend to be someone's boyfriend if I'm an actor in a movie?"

When he put it that way, it didn't seem like lying at all. Technically it still was, but it was okay lying.

Maybe?

"It hardly seems fair that you're paying me, and I'm not paying you."

"Well, I'm hoping to hire you for more than a month. It's a legitimate job. While my grandparents can still take care of themselves, they just need help with some of the things that get harder as you get older."

"I love your gram, and your pap is funny. And you're right. I'm looking for a job." Rose didn't really need to think about it. Maybe it was divine intervention with Derek walking through the door.

Who knew?

But the door was open, and she was going to walk through. "I'll do it."

"That's great. Just let me know when you can start."

"Well, I'm unemployed, so my schedule is wide open. Other than Wednesday and Saturday afternoons and evenings when we have the auction."

"I knew that. If you're available, we can go out to the farm right now."

"I feel like I just put in a good day's work," Charlene said, adjusting her position in her chair and looking at the quilt patches on the table like nothing big had just gone on.

No fake boyfriend had been hired. No employment problem solved.

Maybe, maybe Rose still felt like she was a bit of a reject, and she still didn't feel entirely wanted. But she could almost get excited about the idea of playacting. About pretending to have a boyfriend. About beating her ex at the Dating Game.

And she could definitely get excited about taking care of Derek's gram. A sweet lady, and one she wouldn't mind hanging out with.

"Why don't you come on out, talk to them, and if you're interested, we can talk about your hours and pay."

"That sounds good."

"And then, maybe at some point, we can talk about this whole fake relationship thing, because I guess we'll need to hang out for a few weeks and even maybe get to know each other some so we have a chance of winning the Dating Game."

"That's great. I... I don't really want to play and look ridiculous."

"Me either. I guess I play to win." Derek's eyes glinted. There was humor in them, but there was also a determination. Maybe it stemmed from his personality, or maybe it truly came from the idea that he wanted to beat her ex, just because it would give him a bit of satisfaction as he thought about his own situation.

Whatever it was, Rose was going to take it.

Chapter 4

*Communication, compromise, and always make sure to tell
them that you love them even when you are angry.*
- Samantha Dewar

A little bit bemused at himself, Derek opened the door and held it for Rose to walk through. He couldn't believe he'd just agreed to be this woman's fake boyfriend.

Wasn't that part of the reason he'd been excited to leave the city? To get out of the drama of coworkers and the soap opera that work seemed to become?

Not to mention the added stress when people weren't getting along and when workplace romances bled over and affected daily life and made the workday miserable.

But this wasn't going to do that. It was just a fun thing...

She walked through. He closed the door and said, "You know, I just realized, if we're going to go to my grandparents and talk to them, we're probably going to need to either pretend to be almost engaged or decide that we're going to share with them what's really going on."

She glanced up, surprise on her face. "You're right."

"Maybe we ought to hash out some of these details? So that we're not shocked when people approach us? Or, probably more importantly, so we give out the same story."

"We've agreed to act in the play. Now we have to write it?" she asked, her eyes twinkling a little.

"We need to figure out our own roles anyway."

"Agreed. Do you want to go up and sit in the church sanctuary to talk for a bit? I know they turn the heat down during the week, but it will at least be warmer than outside," she said as a gust of wind blew her ponytail so that it streamed ahead on both sides of her face.

"That's a good idea. It would be a little awkward to do it in the diner," he said, with a little smile, wondering if she would be fine joking about it, or if his words would upset her. He really didn't know what kind of girl she was, even if he'd just committed to being with her exclusively for the next month. He supposed he was going to find out.

To his relief, she grinned. "Unless we really want to make us a soap opera."

"It might end up that way, but we can keep it from becoming that today."

"All right. The back of the church it is then."

They walked around the front, not walking through the basement and bothering the ladies, and walked in the front doors which were always open.

Good to see that hadn't changed in the years that he'd been away. Anyone could stop in the church at any time, to pray, to just talk to the Lord, or to be alone if they needed to.

Or to write the characters that they were going to play for the next month.

He hoped that this wasn't any more of a lie than what he truly thought it was.

Guilt nagged at him some, but he pushed it aside.

They settled on the back pew. She turned to face him a little, tucking one leg up underneath her, and he sat far enough away from her that he could stretch his arm out on the back of the bench and not touch her.

"I'm just wondering who we should tell the truth to and who we should try to pretend with?"

"I don't think we should try to do both. It's going to be too confusing to keep track. Either we're going to be together, or we're not. We'll do it for a month, then the gig will be up, and we'll admit to our close friends and family why we did it, and the rest of the people can just believe we broke up. Amicably, because we'll still be friends."

"All right. That's a lot less confusing. We'll just live with whatever we figure out, and when it's over, it's over. Miss Charlene, Miss Vicki, and Kathy will be the only ones who know along with us."

He could tell that she could see the wisdom in the fewer people knowing, the better, and he was grateful. He didn't want to have to try to figure out who they had told the truth to and who they hadn't. It wasn't something he was used to juggling.

"So, where did we meet?" she asked, tilting her head like he maybe already had the story all figured out.

"I think it would be a good idea to keep everything as close to the truth as possible."

"That makes sense to me. So we met here in Sweet Water?"

"Sure. How about we knew each other beforehand, which is true, and I knew through my grandparents about your situation, which is also true, and when my wife left, we just kind of hit it off." He shrugged, believing with all his heart that the simpler it was, the better. He wasn't going to be able to keep any kind of complicated web of lies straight in his head.

"That sounds good to me. And if they press for details, we'll just have to make them up or say it was a whirlwind romance and we only talked a little bit before we decided we were great together?"

"Wow. I really like it. It's so close to the truth that it will be easy to remember, and I won't feel like I'm lying every time I talk about us. And I guess we could hint around that we're thinking about getting married, but I haven't popped the question. Does that sound good?"

"It does." She ran a hand over her jeans, pleating them and then straightening them out. "How much of our backstories do you think we need to know? I mean, if we haven't been together long, we probably don't need to know a whole lot. And if I'm going to be working out on the farm, we'll probably find some things out naturally, right?"

"That's right. Maybe I can just brush you up a little on my life story, the big events, and you can do the same, and if anybody wants details, we'll just try to put them off. In the meantime, we'll fill in the blanks naturally as we work together."

"That sounds great, and you already remembered that my family owns the auction barn and livestock exchange, and we went to school together, graduating in the same class. And I never left Sweet Water. Although I was married for five years, and I wanted children, and I thought it was forever, and he didn't want kids, and he didn't think it was forever, and he left me for someone who had three children."

"It's crazy how similar our stories are, since my wife didn't want kids either, and she left me for someone who had three kids. He doesn't have sole custody though, so she's not with them all the time. Which is probably a good thing, because she hated kids. At least that's what she claimed. And honestly, she wasn't good with them. I should have known better, but when I broached the topic before we got married, she was open to the idea. In hindsight, I think she was just saying whatever she had to in order to get me to agree with what she wanted me to do."

He'd been pretty bitter about it, for a while, but he found he was able to say this to Rose without the strong feelings surfacing. Almost like...like time was easing the pain, kind of like it promised to do.

He knew it would. It just sometimes didn't feel like it.

"So, would you like to go out Thursday night?" he asked, smirking a little, because it was probably what he was expected to say. But honestly, if he hadn't already agreed to this, he might have been interested anyway. Rose was exactly the type of girl that he wouldn't have looked twice at in high school. She was too down-to-earth, too common, not nearly sophisticated enough for what he had always been attracted to.

But now he knew that sophistication was often just another word for snobbery, and if a person looked down on one thing, they were more than likely to look down on others, things that maybe he didn't want to look down on.

Maybe that didn't make a whole lot of sense, but regardless, he couldn't say he was very interested in someone who took great pleasure in their refined tastes.

Refined tastes were just words that described someone who thought they were better than someone else. And looked down on people who didn't agree with them.

Unfortunately, as an impressionable high school and college student, he hadn't recognized that.

He thought refined meant better.

Now, Rose had a confidence about her that he admired, and her self-effacing sense of humor had been a refreshment from the snobby need for irony and the subtle mockery of others that passed as humor in his circles.

"Why, what a surprise. I'd love to," she said, her eyes twinkling

He found himself wanting to know her because of *her* and not necessarily because of their bargain.

Was that a bad thing?

Could he say that if they decided they wanted to stay together after the month was up, they could?

But she'd be working with his grandparents on the farm.

Maybe it would be best to keep things strictly business, or since strictly business meant having a fake relationship, he wasn't sure exactly where that left them.

"I think this has the potential to get very messy," he finally said. Unable to try to figure out in his head where exactly the lines would be.

"I was thinking about that myself. And I decided why don't we just make sure we're friends? Like, it'll be weird if we forget that this isn't real. So we'll just remind ourselves that we're friends, and we're just doing something goofy for a little bit before we go back to being friends. Does that make sense?" she asked, worrying her lip with her teeth while he watched.

He pulled his eyes away. That was the exact type of thing that he couldn't do. No looking at her lips. No looking at her sparkling eyes and thinking that he might be willing to wake up to those every day.

No thinking that she was the kind of girl that he should have chosen to begin with, rather than someone who put on airs and seemed untouchable.

"The town is going to expect to see us together, so we just have to remember that, and I think I'd really like for us to be able to have a good time. You know? There's no point in doing it if we're both miserable." He was sure about that.

"I agree. This isn't supposed to be more stress, it's supposed to be less."

"That's right." He pulled out his phone, saying, "Do you mind giving me your number? I think that's probably something I should have."

"Right. Not just because of..." Her voice trailed off, then she started with renewed determination. "I'll be working for you."

She rattled off her number, and he typed it in, sending her a text so that she'd have his.

"Got it," she said, smiling at the smiley face he had sent.

"I think we pretty much have things hashed out. I need to get back to the farm, and if you'd like to come out, you're still welcome."

"Yeah. I might as well. I was supposed to work for three more hours anyway. My family's not expecting me. If you don't mind?"

"Not at all." He stood, wondering if he should offer his hand to her but not getting it held out in time before she slid out the other end of the pew.

It might be a little bit of bumping as they figured out the roles, but he actually thought this might work out fine. Not just the idea of her ex getting a little bit of his own medicine, but the idea of spending time with Rose. It would ease his transition back to Sweet Water if he had someone to do things with as he became a part of the community again. It felt like a win-win all around.

Chapter 5

Respect for one another and commitment to each other.
- Jan Newman from Memphis, TN

"Rose, this is my gram, Cordelia," Derek said as they stepped into the warm farmhouse kitchen.

Of course she knew Miss Cordelia from church, but Derek didn't realize how familiar they were, and the polite thing to do was introduce them anyway.

"Just call me Gram," his grandma said, smiling. "And we already know each other. Normally I think you say Miss Cordelia."

"I do, but Gram seems much nicer, especially if I'm going to be spending a lot of time here."

"I knew Derek was looking for someone, but I wasn't expecting him to come back from town with someone in tow already. I've heard that there is a shortage of workers, and the market is tight."

"I think he just had really good timing."

"And the Lord was working things out for him. Maybe He just knew we needed someone and didn't want us to have to wait," Pap said from his chair. "And by the way," he added, "you can call me Pap."

"All right, Pap," Rose said with a smile, glancing up at Derek to make sure he was okay with all of this. He seemed like the kind of guy who was pretty easygoing but wasn't afraid to take charge when necessary.

Sure enough, he had a smile on his face, like he was enjoying their interactions and thinking he made the right choice.

She needed to see a smile like that. After feeling like such a failure for the last couple of days, it was reassuring to know that she could do something right.

God is a rewarder of those who diligently seek him. The verse came to her head without being bidden, and it made her smile.

She knew he didn't reward anyone who told untruths, and she wasn't expecting that. But she had sought the Lord and tried as hard as she could to do what was right.

Maybe this was a reward.

"Are you starting today?" Gram asked.

"We actually hadn't talked about my hours, other than I'd be around when you needed me."

"How many hours were you working at the diner, if you don't mind me asking?" Derek said, and she shrugged. Of course she didn't mind him asking. In fact, that was something he probably should know.

"I had worked up to forty, sometimes more in December, when people were out more. January and February are notoriously slow, just because of the cold weather and all the snow. I've been down to about twenty per week."

"Gram?"

"I had wanted to get the spare room cleaned out, and there were some things in the attic I wanted arranged. In the spring, I'd like to have some help with the garden too. Are those things you think you might be interested in?" Gram asked.

"Sure. I'm here to do whatever you want."

"I just wasn't sure whether you were talking manual labor, or if you want to sit and chat, maybe quilt a little."

"I'm not a very good quilter, but whatever you need done, I'm happy to help with."

With that settled, they decided that Rose would stay for a little while, carrying some laundry up and taking a look at the things that Gram wanted done. They decided on her schedule for the week, and she would keep track of her hours, checking with Gram each week as she made out her schedule for whatever worked for both of them.

"If you guys have everything settled, and you're planning on staying here for a bit, I'm going to run out and fix that water line now that I have the parts I need," Derek said, putting his hand on the doorknob.

She met his eyes. Maybe he saw the questions in hers, because he dropped his hand from the doorknob and turned back.

"Actually, Gram, Pap, there's something we probably ought to tell you."

Gram said, "Oh?" while Pap turned in his chair to more fully face them.

He looked at Rose and didn't seem to know where to start. They were his grandparents, and she figured it wasn't her place. But more than that...she just couldn't.

She couldn't lie. She couldn't tell them that they were a couple when they really weren't.

It seemed great when they were talking about it and fun to playact, but...she just couldn't.

Maybe Derek was having the same issue, because finally he shook his head.

She took that as a sign that it was up to her to go forward. After all, she was the one who had spouted the lie to begin with.

Taking a deep breath, she turned to his gram and looked her straight in the eye.

"At the sweethearts' banquet, I told a lie."

Derek took a breath in, like either he was shocked or he wanted to say something. She didn't give him the chance. But kept talking.

"I saw my ex and his wife sitting there, looking all happy and in love, and it hurt."

That was the truth. It wasn't that she was still in love with her ex, necessarily, she just... Just after everything he'd done, it hurt to see him happy, with someone, and in love, having everything she'd ever wanted, while she had nothing. Because she'd put everything she had into her relationship with him. And he'd betrayed her.

She shook those thoughts off.

"I... I don't usually lie, but somehow the words came out, and I didn't stop them. I said I was in a relationship with someone, a very happy, serious relationship on the verge of getting engaged."

She kept her eyes on his gram, who didn't turn a hair when she admitted that she lied.

She could hardly respect herself for doing it. God abhorred lying, and she spent most of her life feeling the same way. If someone lied, they couldn't be trusted.

"I didn't correct it, but I let the lie sit there. I let them all believe that I was in a happy relationship." She shrugged. "The evening ended without me saying anything or correcting it at all." She took a deep breath. "So, this morning, Derek and I ended up at the church at the same time with the quilting ladies, and they suggested we have a fake relationship. I wanted to do that so much, because I didn't want to have to admit to the whole town that I'd lied. I would look...weak. Like I was still in love with my ex. Like I was jealous. Like I didn't have any character and couldn't find a man on my own, so I had to make it up." She shook her head. "Like having a fake boyfriend is somehow better, I guess. I just didn't want to have to say that it wasn't true. So I jumped on the whole fake boyfriend thing, and reluctantly, Derek agreed to it."

"You asked Derek to be your fake boyfriend?" Pap asked, sounding confused. This was definitely a woman's invention, way too convoluted for a man's normally straight and analytical mind.

"I did," she admitted. "He wasn't too keen on the idea—"

"I agreed. I agreed to do it, and I still will."

She glanced up to see his eyes on her. She couldn't really read what was in them, but she thought maybe pity. Which she hated. But also perhaps a little admiration, and she could only think it was because she didn't want to carry the lie any further.

"I would do it, because in the short time I've been around her, Rose has been the kind of person that I admire and respect and like at the same time. But also because I've been there. I've had my spouse walk out on me. I've had her be with someone else and look happy, while I wasn't. And I resented the fact that I had put everything into our marriage, while she had put everything into a relationship with someone else, so I was left with nothing but rubble, while she stepped into a completely new relationship that she'd been building instead of working on ours."

Rose nodded. That was exactly right. They were supposed to be working on their relationship together, but instead, he'd already had one foot out the door, building something with someone else. She hadn't even known.

She had suspected, and now she felt foolish in a way, but why should she? He was the foolish one. He was the one who hadn't done what he said he would. She just assumed that the man would keep his word. Was it terrible to expect one's spouse to be honest?

She kinda felt the world had things backward. That should be the norm. And when someone didn't do what they said, they should be the ones who were considered the fool. Instead of the person who believed them.

That wasn't the way it was, and there was no point trying to fight the tide. But she appreciated Derek putting into words the way she felt.

"I've never been there," Gram said slowly, looking over at her husband of more than a half-century. "But I can see how painful that trail might be. When you trust someone, and instead of them working with you, they're working with someone else." She tilted her head to the side, speaking slowly like she was thinking as she spoke.

And Rose felt it again. That little slimy curl of jealousy that made her wish that she didn't know what it was like to be betrayed, what it was like to be putting everything into a relationship with someone only to have them turn and decide they'd rather be with someone else. To feel like she'd helped build the man that he'd become, and rather than returning the favor, supporting her and helping her become better, he gave the better person he had become to someone else.

Like he had taken what she poured into him and given it to someone else.

It hurt.

But suddenly, right there in the kitchen, a thought came to her that was so profound, she almost gasped.

Isn't that what God did?

Didn't he pour everything into her? Didn't he love her uncon-ditionally, help her become a better person, a better human, and instead of giving Him her life, living it for Him, she took what He'd given her—her money, her time, her health—and used it on other things.

She had to think about that. Because she could see a lot of similarities. If she pledged her life to Christ but walked away, setting her attention on other things, did that hurt God the way it hurt her when Harry had pledged his life to her and yet got distracted by someone else and walked away with them?

It made her see her relationship with the Lord in a completely different way. Made her see His long-suffering toward her as requiring the patience it truly did.

Made her see how she'd been hurting the Lord and not even meaning to.

Made her long for forgiveness and grace from God and realize that Harry deserved the same from her. She couldn't expect God to forgive her for her walking away from Him, not being completely devoted to Him, if she couldn't forgive Harry.

It was a much greater sin for her to ignore her Creator than for Harry to betray her.

She shook her head, realizing everyone in the kitchen was watching her. Sifting back through her thoughts, she remembered that they'd been talking about the fake relationship that she and Derek were supposed to have.

"I'm sorry, Derek. I know we had everything worked out, but I just don't think I can lie to people. Your gram is just like all the other ladies in the church. I can't look them in the eye and pretend to be something I'm not. Not when I'm in my rational mind. Maybe if I'm green with jealousy or hurt so bad it feels like my whole body is bleeding, but now, when it's just a small pain that feels like it's never going to leave thumping in my chest, I can't do it. I'm sorry."

Derek nodded. And the pity was gone from his eyes, and she was almost positive admiration was there instead. "I appreciate that, because I was having a hard time finding the words. I could have followed your lead, but I couldn't look my grandparents in the eye and lie to them. I... It's good to know that you can't either."

"I'm glad to know you guys have such a tough time lying," Gram said, her tone a little more cheerful than it had been, seeming to say *let's put this stuff behind us*. "But I have an idea. One that I can't believe you guys haven't thought of."

They both turned to her, staring at her, and Rose, at least, was turning things over in her head, wondering what in the world she hadn't thought of that his gram thought was such a great idea.

"What's that?" Derek said, shifting and taking a couple of steps which put him closer to Rose, almost as though he were going to stand with her in solidarity.

He wasn't quite beside her, but she appreciated the proximity. Not sure if he did it on purpose, but it didn't really matter. It still made her feel better, thinking he was on her side.

"Why don't you guys date for real? That would pretty much negate any reason to have to lie. I mean, you might have to still admit that you aren't as close as what you insinuated, but if you're in a relationship," Gram shrugged her shoulders, "you don't have to tell everybody when that started."

"Or I could just admit that I had lied then, but I am in a relationship now?" Rose said, not wanting to have any lie hanging over her head for the rest of her life.

"There you go. You have to admit to the lie, but then there's truly a relationship. And people will be more interested in that gossip than they will be in any confessions."

"That's true." She laughed a little.

People were always interested in gossip, and ladies especially were always interested in who was dating who. She hadn't really been a part of that rumor mill for most of her life, and now all of the sudden, she found herself front and center.

But it wasn't just her.

She looked him in the eye. "I wouldn't ask that of you. I've already dragged you around, switching this way and that, agreeing to do it, backing out, I couldn't blame you at all for wanting to wash your hands of me. And it's only been a morning."

"It hasn't been bad. And we have to do the Dating Game for Miss Charlene anyway. I'm fine with real dating for the next month."

It sounded like he still wanted an end date on it, so she agreed to it immediately, to ease his mind. Not wanting him to think that he was going to be stuck with her for the rest of his life if he agreed to spend a month with her.

"That's sounds like a great compromise. We'll have an end date, one month from today, or after the Dating Game, whichever. We don't have to have a big breakup. We can just quit dating and stay friends?"

That last came out kind of like a question, because she wanted to make sure he was okay with it. They hadn't really been friends to begin with. But she admired him. He'd been honest, and he understood what she was going through, better than anyone she'd ever met. Plus, he obviously respected his grandparents, and while he'd been lured away by the city, he'd come back to his roots and seemed to want to settle down and be a part of the community.

There was a lot to admire in him. She would be honored to be his friend.

"Yes. I definitely would like to stay friends. After all, I just moved back, and I could use some around here."

"Then you can consider me your friend," she said, knowing that friendship was more than just considering someone as such. It involved action, just as much as love did.

"Now that sounds about right," Gram said, and Pap grunted his agreement.

"I'm not sure I understand all about these games. That's not the way we did it when I was young. I told your gram I liked her and wanted to marry her, and that was pretty much it." He spoke with finality.

"That's not quite the way I remember it," Gram said with a little smile.

"I can't help it if you remember wrong," Pap said, but his grin gave him away. Their story might be interesting. It probably was, and Rose hoped that as she worked with them, maybe she'd hear it.

"It's probably not the way I would choose to do things either, but I don't see anything wrong with it, and it's not exactly a hardship to spend time with Rose. So far, she's made my life a whole lot more interesting."

"And complicated," Rose said, her brows raised.

"Complications are to be expected," he said, and he lifted a hand, almost as though he was going to...pat her on the head? Touch her shoulder? She wasn't sure.

But he dropped it and then walked back to the door. "I think we have that settled, so now I'm going to go out and fix that pipe."

"You go right ahead. We'll have something hot to eat when you come in," Gram said before Derek turned the knob and walked out.

Chapter 6

Communication, quality time, and understanding your
spouse's needs and inner workings.
- Jessica Lowery from MO

"Are you sure you don't want me to go home with you? You don't have to face this by yourself if you don't want to."

Derek stood outside on his front porch, his gloved hand on the porch post, looking at her with that intense gaze that he had. The one that made her feel like he cared and was listening and wanted to help all at the same time.

"No. It'll be fine. Talking to my family will be hard. They'll all understand why I did what I did, and I know my sisters will be ecstatic that I'm actually seeing someone, even if it's only for a month."

She grinned, thinking about how many times her sisters had encouraged her to get out and look for someone. They'd known her entire life all she'd wanted was to be a wife and mom. She'd played with dolls, babysat as much as she could, and gotten married young, thinking she would start a family and finally fulfill her dream.

They wouldn't be excited, though, if she told them it was only for a month. After all, that was hardly going to fulfill any dreams.

But they would definitely be happy that it would seem like she was finally moving on.

"All right. If you need me, you have my number. We're still on for Thursday night?"

"We are." She wanted to tell him that if he wanted to come to the auction Wednesday night, he was welcome. After all, if they were truly dating, and he wanted to see her, he could see her there.

But she didn't. She'd grown up around it, and while it was just part of her ordinary, regular life, she also loved it. Loved the auctioneer in the background, loved the excitement in the air, loved seeing old friends and family, seeing people coming, not even planning on buying anything, just for their Wednesday evening entertainment.

She looked forward to sale days, even though they were hard. Even though she worked in the heat and the cold, sometimes getting pretty beat up by animals that were unpredictable. Sometimes witnessing sad partings that tore at her heart.

Sometimes so exhausted by the end of the night, well after midnight, that it was all she could do to drive herself home and take a shower before collapsing into bed.

Still, she'd grown up not knowing anything else, and she loved it. If Derek were her true boyfriend, she would expect him to love it too. Or at least put some effort into liking it.

But since they were only committed for a month, a tenuous tie at best, she wasn't going to say anything.

She drove home, her lie feeling heavy on her heart, knowing that her sisters and mother had surely heard that she had announced she was in a relationship.

She'd taken one look at her phone, read a few texts, before she'd put it right back down. There were all kinds of unanswered texts. From pretty much every one of the ladies in her family.

Her brother Coleman had even texted. His had been short and to the point: **Why are you lying?**

It kind of irritated her that he assumed that she couldn't possibly be with someone. Even though he was right.

Regardless, she hadn't answered anyone because she didn't want to have to repeat herself a hundred times.

Not to mention, she didn't want to spend an hour answering texts before she even managed to pull out of Derek's lane.

So much had happened since she'd been fired from the diner. She'd have to tell them about that, too, if they didn't already know.

It was a small town, and being that people congregated at the sale barn and were in and out of the livestock exchange on a daily basis, her family had probably already heard the rumors.

Pulling into her house just after six, she noted that most of her siblings' vehicles were there.

Her mom's big dualie was parked along the house, hooked to the trailer the way it usually was, and she was glad to see it.

Her mom was the one person she'd texted, right after she'd been fired. She'd promised to tell the story when she got home.

When she walked in, her three sisters, her oldest brother Coleman, and her mom all sat at the table, supper in front of them, and they all turned and stared at her.

Marigold, who had just gotten married to her childhood friend, Dodge, last summer, was the only one who wasn't there.

"We were just talking about you," her mother said, sounding regal. For all she drove around hauling cattle and other livestock all over the place, her mom had a way of speaking and walking that just almost screamed class and decorum.

Her tone indicated she might have been requesting that Rose look at samples of fine china and report to her butler on the pattern she preferred.

It was a tone that made it impossible for Rose to attempt to change the subject or put anything off.

Not that she would.

Her mother's hair, brown and wavy, fell around her shoulders in careless curls.

Her mother was a natural beauty. Even now, in her fifties, she looked young with laugh lines that only emphasized her classic good looks.

Good looks could be deceiving, because her mother was tough, and unafraid, and could outwork any one of her children, including Coleman.

"I guess I have a few things I need to talk to you guys about. So, if you don't mind?"

Coleman's mouth twitched. Normally he was quite serious and didn't joke at all, but she supposed it was an understatement that she had something she needed to say.

Just the fact that he was here eating indicated they'd been expecting this.

Her sisters, other than Marigold, all still lived in the house they'd grown up in.

She'd moved back in when Harry had left her. Maybe she should have stayed in the house they'd bought together. Or maybe she should have found her own place. But maybe she just needed a place where she could nurse her wounds and heal the hurt. If that were possible.

Her two younger sisters, Lavender and Orchid, twins who were only a year younger than Glory, the next sister in line, looked at each other, not even trying to contain their grins.

She didn't wait for Glory to join the twins but jumped right in. "I was fired from the diner today."

She pulled out her chair and sat down. She was going to be here a while. Might as well be comfortable.

"I wondered if that were true. You texted me, but I just couldn't believe it." Her mother's eyes narrowed. "You seem like you're okay."

"I am. It wasn't because of anything that I did wrong. She has family coming, and she needs to give her niece a job, and she doesn't need two people, because the diner is just not that busy this time of year."

"If you were fired at the diner this morning, what have you been doing all day?" Coleman's deep voice was low and serious, not accusing but straight to the point as he always was.

"Well. That's the other thing I need to say."

"Forget about all of that," Orchid said, giving Coleman a derisive glance. "We want to know who it is that you're almost engaged to!"

"If you're actually engaged," Coleman said, lifting a brow and giving her a look before putting the last spoonful of meat in his mouth.

Their mother looked at Coleman. "Son. We talked about this." Her tone held a small warning, and Coleman lifted his eyes, bowing his head before her, like he was giving her deference. Which he always did.

He was too fiercely independent to live under her roof though. Probably the reason that they could get along was because he had moved out. Everyone said he was just like their dad, and from what Rose remembered, it was true. That was probably one of the main reasons why he and her mother needed to be separated in order to get along. Opposites might attract in a romantic sense, but between parent and child, it could make for some testy fights.

Her mother had too much class to get into a low-down, drag-out, shootout fight with one of her kids, but Coleman had tested her patience on more than one occasion before he'd left.

He still ran the livestock auction and the exchange, and they worked together just fine.

That little bit of distance making it possible.

"I lied," she said, looking straight at Coleman, because she knew he'd gloat over the fact that he'd been right.

He surprised her there, because while there was a small flash of satisfaction in knowing that he'd guessed correctly, he didn't look at anyone to prove his point or to taunt. Instead, his look immediately became concerned.

"I've never heard you lie in my life. I want to know why. And why about that?" he said, in the same low, serious tone he'd been using the whole time.

"Well, that's the thing. Harry and his new wife were there last night, and they weren't gloating or anything. Not really, but I guess in a conversation with them, in order to make myself look better and not like a pathetic loser who couldn't find anyone who would take me after Harry left me, and not wanting Harry to think I'm sitting here pining over him, I said I had someone else, and we were close to being engaged." She held her hands out, like *there you go. That's the truth. All of it.*

"And you told them you were kidding immediately?" her mother prompted. She probably got her absolute abhorrence for any type of lie from her mother. They just had never been tolerated in her house. Ever.

"No. That's the problem. I didn't. I should have, I knew that as the words were coming out, but I didn't."

"Then there was that kid that got bit by the dog. Other people probably forgot about you when that happened."

Rose nodded at Glory, appreciating her insight. "That's exactly right. I don't think people are used to having the paramedics at the sweethearts' banquet, and it kinda distracted everyone for a while."

"Distracted them until this morning, when they remembered they had no clue who you were almost engaged to, and everyone wanted me to tell them. And I didn't know what to say!" Lavender said, giving Orchid a glance, and they nodded together.

They were maternal twins, identical. And honestly, sometimes Rose had trouble telling them apart.

Sometimes identical twins had distinctive characteristics, and Lavender and Orchid did, but a person had to really pay attention, and even now in their twenties, it was easier to tell if one saw them together.

Although, when they were separated, sometimes their personalities gave them away. Lavender was much more outgoing. Orchid was quiet and thoughtful and maybe a little bit more of a dreamer. She had a tendency to do kind things in the background, not wanting attention for herself and enjoying being anonymous.

Rose supposed that growing up in a family with five other siblings, being anonymous was something the youngest might have to get used to.

"So you're not dating anyone," Glory stated. It probably should have been a question, but she spoke it like it was a fact. Like they'd already decided it and needed to move on after they got the facts down.

"Well. That's where things got a little hairy." Did she need to talk about the fake relationship?

Yeah. She better tell it all, that way if they heard it from someone, they'd have her side of the story.

She gave a quick rundown of what happened with the ladies at the church and how Derek and she had decided to have a fake relationship.

"Derek Fields? He just moved in with his grandparents? He's thinking about buying their farm?" Coleman interrupted her when she mentioned Derek.

"Yes. That Derek. I graduated with him. He was in my class."

"Yeah. I remember him. He had a couple of sisters and a brother, I think. I remember them as a good family. Even though the parents are living somewhere in the South."

"Yeah. I suppose I ought to know how many brothers and sisters he has, but I don't."

"So are you dating him, or aren't you?" Lavender said, her nose scrunched up.

"I am. We decided that when it came time to confess to his grandparents... I guess I didn't tell you that he offered me a job working as basically a personal care aide to his grandparents."

"Wow. Lose a job in one day and come into another one. You're good," Glory said, grinning at her sister.

Rose smiled back. She didn't feel good. The Lord had been good to her, giving her a job to replace the one she'd lost.

Even if the rejection still stung.

"Regardless, I was going to be out there with his grandparents, so they were going to be the first ones that we would have to lie to, but when it came time to say that we were practically engaged, neither one of us could get that lie out to his grandparents."

"I should hope not," her mother interjected. Sometimes her mother's high standards had been hard to live up to, and she probably spent more time than she should have worrying that she'd let her mom down.

But at the same time, she appreciated those high standards, because they let her know that there *was* a standard. She couldn't imagine living with no standards, just doing whatever she felt like and believing that whatever she thought was right was actually right. The idea that she herself could call something right just because she felt it was almost unthinkable.

Her mother had made sure that none of her children had lived in a fairy tale like that.

"So when we confessed everything to his grandparents, his gram suggested we make the lie truth. By actually dating."

She shrugged. It sounded simple, but the lines as to where that ended were a little more complicated. As she had discovered when she had the little debate with herself as to whether she should suggest to Derek that he come to the auction tomorrow night.

"You still have to confess that you lied. It's not like you can cover it up with the half-truth," her mom said. Her eyes were concerned, but compassion sat on her face as well. It wasn't that her mom didn't think that was going to be a hard thing.

"I know. The guilt I feel for lying won't allow me to just let it go. The next time I see Harry and Leah, I'll let them know. The ladies at the church already know."

"That's my girl," her mom said, making her feel like she just accomplished something hard, even though she hadn't actually done anything.

Her mom wasn't going to follow up on her. She would trust her to do what was right, and she would love her no matter what. That was something that Rose was completely sure of.

"You're dating him, but not because you like him. Just because you're making a lie truth?" Coleman asked, his male brain unable to figure out why exactly that made everything okay. Or why they'd do it to begin with.

"Yeah. Pretty much," Rose said, tired of trying to explain everything. Not sure she understood it herself but knowing she was content with what she was doing and willing to let things play out. "I guess I kinda forgot to tell you guys about the Dating Game."

"That's my favorite church event of the year!" Lavender exclaimed. Then she grinned self-consciously. "I don't know why. I never have a date that I can even apply to be a contestant. Even though it always looks like so much fun."

"It's fun to watch everyone realize how much they don't know about their significant other," Glory said with a mischievous look on her face. "Of course, that makes me think that if I ever have a significant other, I'm going to want to know him front and back, just in case we ever get stuck in the Dating Game."

"Yeah. So that would be a reason for us to date for the next month. Because we agreed to be in the Dating Game."

"You could probably back out," Coleman suggested.

"I guess we could. But the ladies want us to do it. Miss Charlene was rather insistent, and I don't want to let them down. They'd been so ready to support us in whatever we did."

Maybe that wasn't the only reason, but Rose didn't want to examine her motivations to find out that there was more to it than just wanting to not let the ladies down.

Maybe she liked Derek a little more than what she wanted everyone to know.

Chapter 7

Put God first, then spouse, and let spouse feel cherished.
- Elaine Huff from Colbert, GA

D erek stood at the back of the auction arena, hands in his pockets, looking down the steep bleachers into the pit where the animals would be led in and out.

It hadn't started yet, but they were getting ready.

Coleman, Rose's brother who managed the auction, stood on the floor, his head tilted up, talking to the auctioneer who stood in the elevated box, leaning over the railing and discussing something earnestly with Coleman.

When Derek had been growing up, the auction had been much smaller and usually just in the summer, once a week maybe, and even then, he seemed to remember it being sporadic.

But in the ten or fifteen years since Coleman had taken over, he'd turned it into something that was a draw for farmers for miles around.

That was according to his grandparents, who hadn't come tonight because, even though it was warmer than it had been, it was still too cold for them to want to go out.

Not to mention, the auction usually lasted until after midnight, and they didn't want to be out so late.

His gram had given him that look that grandmothers everywhere tended to have and said that she thought that maybe he'd want to be there until it was over.

It was almost like she thought he truly liked Rose and was dating her because he wanted to. She'd forgotten that they had just agreed to it, more because of the Dating Game than anything.

"Haven't seen you around for a while," a voice said beside his ear.

He looked over to see Calhoun Powers, one of the six Powers brothers, the family who owned the trucking company and feed store outside of Sweet Water. He'd graduated with Calhoun along with Rose.

If she wanted to have a fake relationship, Calhoun would have been a good one to ask. He'd been around Sweet Water all his life, never left.

Rose had to know him fairly well.

"Yep. My grandparents and I are talking about me buying the farm. I'm here to stay," he said, turning and grabbing Calhoun's proffered hand.

"Good to hear it. Lots of people leave and never come back, but some of you guys get smart," he said with a grin.

"Yeah, took me ten years or so, but eventually I figured it out," he said. If Stephanie hadn't left him, he'd still be in The Cities. No point in saying that. Because he'd been unhappy.

"Well, at least you figured out the place to be on Wednesday night in Sweet Water. Gotta try the cheese fries, they're good," Calhoun said, lifting the boat of fries dripping in golden yellow cheese sauce that he held in his other hand and sticking one in his mouth.

"I'll do that. This is the first time I've been here since it got so big. My grandparents are telling me it's quite a thing now."

"Yeah. Coleman has really done a great job with it. He gets all the credit, but his sisters are here every time the doors are open, working in the back. Typically auction houses don't have dependable help like that. But it's a family thing."

"I suppose those are the best kinds of things," Derek said, thinking that that's how he'd thought his family was going to go when he got married.

He supposed he didn't have any grand dreams or plans, just a general sense that they'd have kids, they'd grow up, and they'd all be a big happy unit together. Working together in whatever they did.

"Coleman is in charge here, but the sisters help. None of the girls except Rose ever moved out." He said that kind of offhandedly, not as an insult exactly, just acknowledging the fact that most families didn't stay together, live together, after the children graduated from high school.

Derek knew that wasn't exactly a modern way of doing things, but he didn't really see why it was such a negative. So many times, families split up because they just couldn't get along.

It was refreshing to see a family who pulled together, whose egos didn't get in the way of wanting success for everyone.

He didn't know how Rose and her sisters actually felt about each other, but just the fact that they still were working together, living together, told him that there was some serious character in those sisters.

"I don't know if you heard, but my brother Dodge married Marigold, now he's here every Wednesday night, only instead of watching, they've got him down there working." Calhoun laughed and ate another cheese fry.

Calhoun must not have heard the latest gossip. Not surprising, since he'd probably been working, not hanging around chewing the fat with anyone.

Derek figured he wouldn't be the one to enlighten him. But probably by the end of the evening, he'd have heard something and realized that Derek might well be down there helping. Maybe even expected to.

"I doubt it's a hardship. I actually always kind of wanted to do that. Maybe not every week, but it seemed like a fun job, moving animals around, organizing them after they're sold, and loading them up and moving them out. A real service for farmers."

"Yeah. You're right about that. I've helped a few times, and it's really not bad work. Maybe in the heat of the summer, it gets a little exhausting, but that might explain why those girls aren't married. The fella knows that if he latches on one, the whole family ends up coming with her."

Derek figured he probably was insane, because he hadn't even thought about that.

Hanging out with Rose was one thing, but being attached to her, as in married, would mean marrying into that family.

Of course he hadn't thought about it, since he hadn't thought about marrying Rose or anything even close. Just a fake relationship.

He saw her then, through the open doors of the arena, following a big horned bull, out beyond the scale on the other side of the ring. The bull was moseying along, and Rose, her hair put up in a ponytail, wearing a coat and carrying a cattle rod, walked behind him. Her attention was on the bull until someone yelled at her, and she looked over, waved her hand, and yelled something back.

He was too far away to hear the actual words, but he didn't need to. They were just making sure they had a place for everything and sticking it all in the right area.

He didn't like to see her taking her attention off the bull though.

There were plenty of areas to get away, if the bull decided to change his mind and turn around, although a person had to be ready for it.

The fences weren't super high, and she could easily step up and vault over.

He was sure she'd probably done it before. A person couldn't work with cattle as much as she had to and not get chased over a fence once in a while.

It came with the job, but for some reason, it didn't sit well with him.

Probably because she was so slight, no match for the bull she followed, and it didn't seem like a fair contest.

Or maybe because he knew her a little bit, knew she was kind and helpful, and didn't want to see her get hurt.

Regardless, there was a part of him that wanted to leave his conversation with Calhoun, and take that cattle prod from Rose, and chase the bull himself.

Calhoun was talking about the price of grain and how that was affecting agriculture in general, and he listened with half an ear.

It was all stuff he needed to know, and that would be the main reason he would come to the auction, aside from possibly getting a good price on an animal that might improve his herd. It was all about networking, knowing who was selling and who was buying and what the prices were.

In his corporate job, that was all done online, but out here in North Dakota, it was still a face-to-face, people talking to people kind of thing.

"I think the rumors are true," Calhoun said, sticking a fry in his mouth and chewing thoughtfully.

Derek had only been paying partial attention, but that comment made his head jerk around.

Calhoun smiled, like a cat with a bird feather in its mouth.

"What rumors?"

"Wow. That caught your attention faster than old biddies at a tea party." He grinned. "Being in the city made you a glutton for gossip?"

"It ruins a man." His words were only half joking. City living did make a person soft. He'd known that the day he'd come back to North Dakota and walked out with the hired man on his grand-parents' farm to feed the animals. He'd been cold the second they stepped out and practically frozen into an ice cube by the time they got back in.

He definitely needed to toughen up.

"So you and Rose are together?" Calhoun said casually.

"Yeah," Derek said, not even bothering to think about it. Re-alizing he liked the fact that it wasn't a lie, and...other than the automatic shock of having a "someone" to be with, it felt right.

"Then you should be down there helping her. I don't know why you're standing up here." He popped another fry into his mouth and grinned.

"Because the city makes a man soft. I think she didn't want me to get hurt." He was totally making that up, poking fun at himself, but it made him wonder why she hadn't asked him to come. After all, obviously Calhoun expected him to be down there working. Why wouldn't she have said something?

They'd only been together for a day. He had to give her a little slack.

Plus, around here, he figured guys didn't wait for an invitation, they just jumped in and helped wherever they could.

He had been in the city long enough, with everyone minding their own business, no one wanting to stick their nose into someone else's stuff, because it just wasn't done there, that he'd forgotten that around here, people just lent a hand. Didn't even think about it.

"Well, you're not going to get tough standing around up here." Calhoun shoved the last fry in his mouth and balled up the cardboard boat in his hand.

"Standing up here eating cheese fries? I guess you got that right," Derek said, smirking but knowing that if he were truly in a real relationship with Rose, he wouldn't hesitate to go down. Just tell her to put him to work wherever she needed him, but...the fact that theirs was not exactly a real relationship left him in somewhat of a limbo.

Did she even want him here? Maybe that's why she hadn't said anything.

But they had agreed that they would date for a month. Like real date, so they didn't have to lie. So it made sense that he would act the way he would act if he were really dating her.

He couldn't believe he needed Calhoun to point that out to him, but he appreciated it.

"See you around, man." He smacked Calhoun on his shoulder, met his grinning gaze, and strode away. If Rose didn't want him, she was going to have to say so.

Chapter 8

Open communication about everything.
- Cyndi Wannamaker

R ose walked behind four nannies, heavy with pregnancy, moving them out of the way so that when they ran the calves through, the bottom pens would be empty.

Maybe it was because of the break in the weather, finally after six weeks of constant subzero temperatures, or maybe it was just people were tired of the cold and needed to get out. Whatever it was, they hadn't had this many animals since last October.

Normally in the winter, they only had one auction per week. They dropped the Saturday auction sometime in November or December, depending on supply and what prices were doing.

They picked it back up again in the spring when things started to move again. Usually March or April.

With only one option and with the weather being so terrible, she figured it only made sense that tonight was going to be a big night.

They had enough pens, but just barely.

The nannies were going into a pen with five other nannies. They'd be fine for the two hours they'd have to stand together, but normally they tried to keep things separate as much as they could.

Auction barns were known for spreading diseases among animals, especially ones that weren't vaccinated, and they did their best to avoid that whenever possible, penning animals only with the ones from the farms where they came from as much as they could.

"Hey, Rose," Glory yelled from three aisles over. "Put those down on the end. There isn't enough room in that pen, and it'll keep us from having to bring them the whole way back."

"Got it," she said.

Glory and Marigold were the two that usually ran things in the back.

Coleman oversaw everything, and the twins helped wherever they were needed.

Now that Marigold was married, Glory had taken over more, although Marigold probably wouldn't back out completely, not until she had children.

"Can I give you a hand?" a deep voice said behind her, and her stomach twisted, sending shockwaves through her torso, before she even registered who it was.

"We're always looking for good help," she said over her shoulder, keeping the goats moving. That was often the key to keep an animal moving in the direction you wanted to go. If you let it stop, it had time to decide that maybe the direction it was going wasn't the direction it really wanted to go and it would take that opportunity to make a run for something else.

"I kinda figured if we were together, I'd be down here."

"That's true. I'm sorry. I thought about asking, but...I dunno, it just felt like I would be imposing, making you feel guilty if you didn't want to."

"We're together. I agreed to it. Whatever that means."

His words were the right words, and they should have completely reassured her, but for some reason, they didn't. Maybe because she wanted him to be there because he wanted to be, not because he had to keep his promise.

Regardless, she could use the help. She'd been wondering how she was going to get the pen door open, without the other nannies getting out.

"We're putting these down in that far pen, and I need to open the gate somehow, without losing these."

"Is it okay if the ones in the pen come out?"

"Sure. We just need to get them all back in."

"Got it," he said, moving along the side, slowly, while she backed off, allowing the goats to see him as he moved up beside them and went ahead of them, opening the gate to the pen where the other goats were. The other goats immediately came out the opening.

He knew better than to run in front of them but just kind of slid around, not scaring them.

She wanted to sigh. One of those *I'm so glad this is happening to me* kind of sighs. The kind of sigh where she realized immediately she was working with someone who knew what they were doing and were going to make her job easier, not harder.

Of course, goats were one of the easiest animals they worked with.

Too small to really be a danger, except the most fractious nanny, and occasionally an aggressive billy, but typically goats didn't weigh too much more than an adult, and honestly, in all her years of handling them, she'd never been hurt by one.

Unlike pretty much every other animal they handled.

Even geese could be vicious.

They herded the goats back in, easily moving them and shutting the door behind them.

She smiled at him. "Thanks. It's nice to work with someone who knows what they're doing."

He jerked his head. "I was just talking to Calhoun, and I think he was afraid the city had made me soft. He's right, but I guess there are just some things you don't forget, and working with animals is one of them."

"Or maybe if you've done it since you were born, it just kinda comes naturally," she said, shrugging her shoulders. Because there were some people who just never got it. No matter how often they worked with animals, no matter how often they tried, they just didn't get the knack.

"I suppose that's true. Just depends on where you were born and what you were taught as a child. We really don't think about that much, but it's true."

"I think God probably made it that way. Because he expected us to grow up and help our families and our parents and not dive into something completely new. Although, he made us elastic enough that we could if we needed to." It always amazed her how God made humans so adaptable but rigid at the same time.

"That might be true for some people, but I don't think I was ever going to fit in in the city."

"Looked like you were doing okay to me." She wiggled the gate to make sure the latch held before she turned to face him. "You had a good job, were successful. At least that's what I heard around town."

They walked down the aisle. The auctioneer's voice travelled back to them, indicating the auction had started.

They always sold the calves first, and the twins moved them in and out. Just the way they'd always done it, no real reason. But moving the calves around was tough, physical work, and once that was done, Glory and Rose usually handled the rest of the animals while Coleman worked in the actual auction pit and the twins pitched in where they were needed, usually slipping out early.

Coleman worked the pit because that was the most dangerous place and also the most important one, because it was his job to show the animals at their best as much as possible.

"I have a few minutes. You want to see something neat?"

"Sure." He lifted a shoulder like he couldn't imagine what in the world she would show him at an auction barn.

Maybe he wouldn't care, but she took a chance that he'd be as awed as she was and walked back to the far corner, to the pens that they typically didn't use, unless they were extremely full, like they were tonight.

Still, there were several pens that were empty, and they walked by those, back to the big one in the corner.

"She just had them today," she said, jerking her chin at the sow in the corner with her mass of piglets sleeping on top of each other.

"Wow. They're so tiny."

"I know. Especially compared to her. She must be going on eight hundred pounds." She was just guessing, because they hadn't run her over the scale, but over the years, she'd gotten pretty good at estimating an animal's weight.

Sometimes she'd be way off, particularly in the winter when a winter coat could hide an animal that was actually skin and bones.

But she was pretty confident on that estimate. The sow might even be a little more.

"And I bet those little piglets don't even weigh a pound."

"Probably not," she agreed, content to just watch them. Mom lazed happily, her ears perked up and one eye open as she listened to them talk.

"She hasn't been protective?"

"That's why we have her back here. I know the farmer that was selling her wanted to unload her before she had them. He's getting out of it, since his wife passed away before Christmas, and he just doesn't have the heart anymore."

Sad, but it was also the way a marriage should be. When one spouse died, the other should have been so connected to them that it felt like they'd lost a part of themselves.

"Looks like he should have done it a week ago."

"Yeah. It was so cold though, no one was moving around much. He probably wouldn't have gotten much for her. But now... I think they're going to sell them, but I don't think anyone's going to want to mess with trying to move them, so he's still probably not going to get much out of her. Which is a shame because she's a good mom."

"How many did she have?"

"Fifteen. She laid on one, but it might have been born dead. We couldn't really tell."

"Wow. That's a lot."

"Yeah, and she has the spigots for all of them, so there's really no reason that they shouldn't make it."

He grinned at her use of farmer slang indicating that there were enough teats to feed each piglet.

They stood and watched them for a while, and then he said, "Are you allowed to tell me who brought her in?"

"Sure. Samuel Blackstone. You might not have heard of him, he lives about fifty miles to the west."

"You're right. I haven't, but I think my farm can use a pig," he said.

She loved that. He didn't need a pig any more than she did, but sometimes a person ended up with things that they didn't need, just because they knew it would help someone else out. She loved that he obviously had a heart and could show compassion.

She'd met a lot of men who couldn't.

"I admire that. She'll go last probably, although Coleman said he might sell her before the feeders, just to see if he could get a better price for her."

"I'll try to keep an ear out," he said.

"If I see anyone other than us bringing her out, I'll text you," she said, used to doing those kinds of things. Sometimes people would be out talking and not in the actual auction arena, and if she knew they wanted something, she let them know. It was part of her job really. "Coleman had talked about getting her, but he and Mom are going on a trip later this month, and although my sisters and I can take care of them, he didn't want to add to our workload if he can help it. We'll be doing an auction or two by ourselves."

"I didn't know that. But I can help."

"Rose! We need you up here," one of her sisters yelled at her. She wasn't even sure which one, she just knew her break time was over.

"Come on. I'll let everyone else know you're available, and I'm sure no one will have a problem putting you to work."

He grinned and followed her easily. She really didn't need him to be easy to work with on top of everything else. But as he spent the evening moving animals around and helping to load the ones that had been bought, she realized he truly was.

He took orders well but could make split-second decisions and issue commands just as easily.

Someone like that was hard to find. Oftentimes, people who were leaders couldn't follow. And people who made great followers couldn't make a decision to save their souls.

He did make it in time to purchase the sow, and while he couldn't raise the bid on it, he had asked her to point out Mr. Blackstone, and she saw him slipping him a check, independent of going through the auction house.

She assumed that he was paying him fair market value for his time.

He didn't say anything to her about it though, and she didn't jump him. Just kept that tucked away. One more thing to admire about him.

After the last animal had been loaded and the last car had pulled away, Coleman thanked him and told him to come back next week for a paycheck. Which was the way he paid everyone—they worked this week, got paid the next.

Derek didn't argue, and Rose figured that meant he'd be back next week at least. She was glad he'd allowed them to pay him, since he definitely earned it.

"That was fun," Derek said as they walked out of the dark sale barn, the lights having been turned out as everyone dispersed.

"I love it. It's a lot of work, and sometimes I don't feel like going in on Wednesdays and Saturdays, but I almost always have a good time."

"I can see why."

The wind blew, and even though it was above zero, it was still below freezing, and they didn't linger in the parking lot.

"We're still good for tomorrow night?" he asked as he opened her car door.

"Sure are," she said with a smile.

Glory was already in her seat, since they'd come together, so she didn't mess around but said, "Thanks a lot."

She hoped he knew that she meant for coming in the first place and not just for helping.

He nodded. "My pleasure."

Chapter 9

Trust and communication. My husband is my best friend and that's something that makes our marriage work we tell each other everything and have no secrets from each other.
- Dreaa Drake from Kentucky

Thursday morning came early, but Derek was smiling as he went about the feeding chores, thinking about last night and how much fun it had been.

He would never have said that working at a sale barn would be something he'd enjoy, but he supposed having the right person there made all the difference.

He really couldn't keep the smile off his face.

Even if it had been more difficult to get out of bed this morning, because of the late night.

He wasn't in a big rush, either, because he knew Rose had set up with his grandparents that she would come later on Thursday mornings, because she knew Wednesdays were usually a late night for her.

He and his grandparents had actually scheduled to talk about the sale of the farm before she came.

He really didn't think there would be much to discuss. They'd just name their price and he'd figure out a way to pay it.

He had his share of the money from the sale of his home in The Cities and a little more money that he'd saved.

Before he'd come out, he'd looked at property values, and he knew that he would be in line with what his grandparents should ask if they were asking fair market value, and he didn't want to pay anything less.

He was eager to get talking to them, eager to get started on his future, although he wasn't sure why. It wasn't like he had any big plans, except...he wasn't sure. For some reason, it had become a lot more important to him to have his future settled.

Maybe it had something to do with Rose, but it hardly could.

It wasn't like their relationship was serious. Or going anywhere.

Still, he took a moment to admire the frosty blue sky, painted in oranges and pinks as the sun came up.

Watching the breath from the calves as they ate their feed, and the steam as the sun hit them, and the frost that lay on their coats started to melt and evaporate.

It was a beautiful morning, the wide North Dakota sky, fresh air, cold, crisp, and somehow cleansing.

A hard life. But a good one.

Kind of funny, with as cold as it was, as difficult as the work could be, that the people in North Dakota rated themselves the second happiest in the nation, after Hawaii.

He could understand why though.

Whistling a little, glad he decided to come home, he walked out of the barn and into the house. Later today, he'd need to move some hay bales from the far field to the field where the cows were wintering.

Maybe, if Rose was done with his gram, she'd want to ride along.

The thought surprised him. They weren't really dating.

But... But they were.

He should have known better than to agree to something that was guaranteed to confuse him.

"Good morning," his gram said cheerfully as he walked in the kitchen, warm and toasty and smelling of coffee and bacon.

"Just got a lot better. Smells like someone's cooking bacon, and I know there's coffee."

"I think both are necessary for a good morning, so we try to have them as much as possible," his gram said, breaking eggs into a bowl like she'd known he was on his way in.

Maybe she'd been watching out the window for him.

"Looks like it was about minus ten out there this morning," Pap said.

"Yeah. I thought that cold snap was over, but it definitely dipped down last night."

"The water wasn't frozen, was it?"

"Nope. The heat tape is plugged in and working. I checked it last night after I got back."

"You were out pretty late," his gram said. He returned her grin, shaking his head. Funny, he was in his thirties, and his grandparents were keeping track of what time he pulled in.

He didn't mind. In fact, he actually thought it was kinda nice to have someone care about him.

A wife would too.

The right wife. He'd already been down that road, and he wasn't going down it again without a really good reason.

Rose was a good reason.

He couldn't argue with that. He thought that that was exactly right, and wherever that thought came from, he kind of wanted to take it out and look it over.

Maybe, maybe during the month that they were together, he could try to convince her that they should do it for real.

Except...would she think he was crossing lines? Going past the boundaries they'd set up? Maybe she'd be less than impressed if he didn't respect the barriers they had put in place.

He poured his coffee and set the table, pulling the bacon out of the skillet and pouring some orange juice for Pap while Gram set the eggs on the table.

Pap prayed for the food, and although Derek was expecting to talk about the farm, he figured they'd do that after breakfast was over. But he'd barely said amen when with his fork in one hand, Pap leaned his forearms on the table and said, "We're still going to talk about the farm today?"

"Yes, sir. I'm still interested in buying it, although I want to be clear that whatever happens, you guys are always welcome. I'm not trying to buy it out from underneath you to kick you off of it."

"We know. We would never think that," Gram said, reaching across the table and patting his hand.

"I've been hesitant to broach the subject, because I have to admit something that's kind of hard. Actually very hard," his pap began, his fork still poised in midair. He hadn't even touched his food.

That concerned Derek. What in the world could Pap want to talk about, and why would it seem to be making him too nervous to eat?

"I know you met Bud, our hired guy. He showed you the ropes before he left."

"Yeah. He seemed like an okay guy," Derek said. He hadn't been the kind of guy that Derek would have wanted to hang out with, but he didn't seem like the kind of guy that was going to murder anyone in their sleep, either.

"Well, his family was going through a hard time. His mom had cancer, and long story short, his family was strapped for money. He got it by selling cattle out from underneath my nose. As well as feed and pretty much anything that wasn't nailed down." Pap looked down at the plate before he looked back up. "I shouldn't have trusted him with so much, but I guess with your grandma and I getting older, and my knees and back giving me so much trouble, I just couldn't get out and around like I had been. I couldn't go out and check on him."

"And he seemed so trustworthy that when he offered to go in to the bank and put our deposits in for us, we put him on our account. We thought it would be okay," his gram added, her eyes now looking worried, and her food forgotten.

Something seriously nasty turned in Derek's stomach. Whatever his grandparents were going to say, he was sure he wasn't going to like it.

"I guess what we're saying is the farm is mortgaged, there is not enough feed to make it through the rest of the winter, and I thought we had three hundred head of cattle, but...we don't. We barely have fifty."

Derek pressed his lips together. If he were going to buy the farm, the mortgage wouldn't matter. Gram and Pap just wouldn't get as much money. But he'd wanted a working farm, purchasing everything together, cattle, equipment, feed.

He couldn't make money to pay his mortgage if he didn't have anything with which to make it.

The money he had saved was only going to be a down payment. He couldn't use that to purchase anything, or the bank wouldn't loan him the money to buy the farm.

If the farm were paid off, and he needed to buy cattle and equipment, he could work something out with his grandparents there.

But he didn't have nearly enough to do a down payment and buy everything he needed to start farming. Plus, Gram and Pap wouldn't be as financially secure as he'd thought, and he might need to help them.

"Do you mind if I look at the books? Do you have them straightened out? Are you doing something about this? Prosecuting him or something?"

He looked from Gram to Pap. Both of them looked down at the table.

Finally, Gram looked up. "Bud's mom was a friend of mine. We grew up together. Sure, she moved to a different town and went to a different church, and we barely saw each other, but I still considered her a friend. I couldn't begrudge her son the money to take care of her. Even if he took it without our permission."

Derek just sat there, staring at his grandmother. There was no anger, no bitterness, no anything on her face. Or in her voice. Or in her posture.

"How much did he take?"

"About half a million," Pap said.

This person had taken half a million from them, and neither one of them were going to do anything about it?

"Can you prove it?"

"Oh yeah. He even admits it. But he doesn't have it to pay it back. It went to the hospital."

"How is his mom doing?" He wasn't sure where that question came from. He really didn't care. After all, someone who would steal half a million dollars from two elderly people for his own selfish reasons didn't deserve...

"She died two weeks ago. That's why he quit."

Darek sat, stunned, because he realized exactly why. "He didn't need to steal from you anymore."

"He felt bad. About what he'd done. And he confessed and said he knew he deserved to go to jail. That he came straight from his mother's funeral to tell us that."

Derek stared at his plate. His appetite completely gone.

He knew his grandparents were serious. Knew they wouldn't lie. Knew the man had taken from them more than he could ever repay, and they weren't even going to prosecute, they weren't going to try to get anything out of him, and they were going to let it go.

He couldn't believe it.

Except he could.

This was every bit something that he would expect out of his grandparents. The kind of compassion and love and humbleness they preached, only not with their mouths. They did it with their lives.

This was a huge sacrifice, a huge piece of their retirement, what they'd worked for all their lives, the sweat and the sacrifice and living at the poverty level while working eighteen-hour days spring, summer, and fall, putting up with subzero temperatures most of the winter, always thinking in the end it would pay off.

And now?

This Bud had taken it from them. Rather than honestly finding a way to pay his mother's bill, he cheated his grandparents out of their lifetime of work, the ease that they deserved in their retirement years.

They should have been millionaires.

Instead, they'd be lucky to have enough money to live on for the rest of their lives.

He blew out a breath. He knew better than to try to talk them into anything. It was obvious they were worried about telling him, but they'd already decided on their course of action.

And he would be wrong to talk them out of it.

They were living the Bible teaching they'd always said they believed—*forgive as I have forgiven you.*

Wow.

"I'd really like to see the books, but if you don't mind, first I need to take a walk." He spoke slowly and softly, just in awe. In awe of what his grandparents would do, had done, and looking at his life, he'd never done anything even remotely close to this.

He was angry at his wife for walking out.

She hadn't taken his life savings along with her.

And even if she had, he was young. He could work to get it back.

And yet, he had so much trouble forgiving.

"I was afraid you were going to be angry," Gram said.

"Son, I want you to understand—"

"I do. That's just it. You guys humbled me. I'm not even sure I deserve to sit at the same table as you do."

He stood, walking back out, grabbing his coat, and shoving his feet into his muck boots, not wanting to take the time to lace his warmer ones.

Unbelievable.

Chapter 10

My Mom and Daddy were married for 61 years when he passed away. My Daddy always said, God, his wife and children came first. Boy, did he live those words. When my sisters were small he worked two and three jobs so my Mom could be home with us. Once we were at a certain age Mom went to work. We did things as a family. Mom and Daddy would have their "date" night on Friday or Saturday night. HE always treated my Mom as that young girl he felt in love with. He carried a picture of her in his wallet from their honeymoon that with every new wallet that picture when in.
- Millie from New Jersey

Rose walked into the kitchen late, as was usual for Thursday morning.

Wednesdays were always late nights, and no one was ever in a hurry to do anything on Thursday morning.

When the Saturday auction started up again, Sunday mornings were the same. They got up in time to go to church.

However, when she walked into the kitchen, she knew it wasn't going to be a typical Thursday.

First of all, Coleman was there.

He was never there in the morning and definitely not on Thursdays.

She looked at the clock. Ten o'clock.

Later than she usually slept in on Thursdays, but not late enough to warrant Coleman's presence.

All three of her other sisters were there as well, along with her mom.

Her mom was the only one who didn't sleep in on Thursdays.

She couldn't blame her mom; after having lost her husband, with six children to support and a business to run, her mom hadn't had time to sleep.

She worked almost night and day to make sure that what she and her husband had started didn't go under.

"Good morning," her mom said from her place at the foot of the table.

Coleman sat at the head. Glory leaned against the counter, while Lavender and Orchid sat side by side, cups of steaming liquid in front of them. Tea probably, since neither one of them drank coffee.

"Looks like there's a family meeting. Only we're missing Marigold," Rose said, mostly joking.

"She's on her way," her mom said immediately.

That made Rose stop on her way to the counter to grab her own hot water for tea. "Something going on I missed?"

"She had an announcement, and she wanted us all to be here for it. We were just on our way to go up and get you, since Marigold and Dodge should be here any moment."

"I think I just heard their pickup pull in," Coleman said, his voice low and rough, sounding like he hadn't talked too much this morning yet.

With her brows furrowed, Rose turned back to the counter. What in the world could Marigold have to announce that she needed the whole family for?

Maybe they were moving.

That sent a jolt like lightning through her. Shocking and painful.

She didn't want her sister to leave. Didn't want things to change. Didn't want to see the family broken apart.

Maybe it was because of losing her dad, but she loved having her family around and close, and although her dreams of having children and raising them with cousins and aunts and uncles and grandparents all around like a big amazing support system hadn't worked out, that didn't mean she didn't want to be an aunt to her nieces and nephews and still have big family get-togethers, everyone working in the business and getting along.

Maybe Marigold was pregnant.

Excitement caused her lips to turn up and her fingers to tighten on her teacup. Wouldn't that be amazing?

As she turned from the counter, Marigold walked in the door, followed by Dodge. Marigold smiled, almost ear to ear, and looked beautiful, with her rosy cheeks and her bright eyes and the glow that just seemed to shimmer off her since Dodge and she had gotten together.

It made Rose wish she had a best friend that she could fall in love with. Marigold just looked so happy, better than she ever had in her entire life.

Marigold unwrapped her scarf but didn't take her coat off as she walked into the kitchen and looked at everyone sitting at the table, then glanced at Rose who stood over by the counter.

"Wow. When I asked for everyone to get together, I wasn't actually expecting you would listen to me."

"You said you had something you needed to tell us, information. We're all curious," her mom said, not sounding worried, exactly, but Rose thought maybe her mom was thinking some of the same things she was.

Was Marigold leaving? Would the family be broken apart?

Surely her mom knew change happened, but probably she didn't want it any more than any of her kids did.

Maybe even less.

"Well then, we'd better not keep them waiting," Dodge said, slipping his arm around Marigold's waist and pulling her to his side. It was a gesture of love but also of protection and possession.

Marigold's arm went around him, and they stood there shoulder to shoulder as Marigold opened her mouth and said, "We were just at the doctor's yesterday afternoon. That's why we were late to the auction. We're expecting. Twins."

Her smile grew even bigger, excitement causing her voice to tremble, as Dodge stood, looking excited and proud and happy and not the slightest bit scared or anxious.

Lavender was the first to jump up, squealing and running over to Marigold. "I knew it! I knew that's what you're going to say! Oh, this is so exciting! I'm going to be an aunt!"

Glory went over as well, hugging Marigold, as Dodge slipped away, giving the sisters room to congratulate his wife.

Rose made her way over, excitement the dominant emotion in her chest, but to her dismay, there was something else there too. Something heavy and dark. Something that felt almost evil.

Jealousy.

She had been the one who had dreamed all of her life of having children. She had been the one who had played with dolls, named everything, mothered everything, babysat every kid she could get her hands on, even without pay.

She'd wanted nothing more for her life than to be a wife and mother, and yet...her arms were empty. Her husband gone. And now her sister... Her sister who she loved was going to have not one baby but two!

So maybe her steps were slightly slower, and maybe that's why she saw her mom.

It was an odd look on her mom's face. Excitement, happiness, pride for sure, but there was something else. Maybe it was how her eyes slipped to Dodge, and something very much like regret entered them.

Rose wasn't sure whether she was seeing it correctly or not, but the look reminded her that the The Piece Makers Quilting Club had tried to set her mom up with Dodge's father, Mr. Powers.

They seemed like the perfect couple. He'd lost his wife, she'd lost her husband, and their families were both heavily involved in Sweet Water agriculture.

They were very similar in age, had similar interests, and would complement each other beautifully.

But it had been the most spectacular failure that the Sweetheart Sewing Circle had had to date.

And that was saying something.

Something about the look in her mother's eyes said maybe she regretted it.

Then the look was gone, and her mom was hugging her sister and congratulating her along with everyone else, and Rose added her voice into the mix, shoving aside the nagging voice that said it wasn't fair.

Life wasn't fair.

Even as she hugged her sister, the Bible verse popped into her head: *God is a rewarder of those who diligently seek Him.*

Wasn't He?

It seemed like she tried to do right all her life, to be a good daughter, good sister, good person to seek God and do His will. Knowing that His will for her life was for her to do right, to seek peace and pursue it.

Where's my reward? Where's my child? My children? Why did you put this deep longing in me, if you weren't going to give me children?

No answer. She hugged her sister tighter, happy but also miserable.

As she pulled back, Glory met her eyes from the other side of Marigold. There was understanding and maybe a little pity in them.

The twins had been in their own little world growing up a good bit of the time, and of course Coleman had been a part of the family, but as a boy, he'd been different. He was their protector, and they loved him, but he wasn't always privy to the girl things they talked about. He certainly had never shared a room with them, hadn't had the late-night chats, the discussions about the things they loved and how situations should be handled.

Marigold and Glory and she had been close. And now that Marigold was married, Glory probably understood her better than anyone else in the family.

That's what she read in her gaze—that she understood and felt bad, even while she was happy for her other sister.

Rose pushed the nasty feeling in her chest away, swallowing. She lifted her chin and gave a tremulous smile. Glory lifted her brows, almost in inquiry, without words. Rose didn't need them. She shook her head just a little and forced her smile to grow larger.

They stepped back, their eyes on Marigold as she practically hummed with excitement and anticipation.

Truly, Rose didn't feel anything but happiness *for* Marigold. And, she reminded herself, sometimes God's timing wasn't hers. Which meant maybe her day was coming.

Chapter 11

No.1: Faith in God! No. 2: Mutual respect and lots of love No.
3: Sharing the load of work
- Debbie Jones from Hartselle, AL

D erek had seen Rose pull in around dinnertime. He'd texted
to let them know he wasn't going to the house for lunch. Part
of the reason was he was still so amazed at what his grandparents
had done.

But part of the reason also was he needed to think.

He hadn't expected to be handed the farm, but he had expected
to have enough cattle and crops and equipment included in the
purchase that it would be a turnkey operation for him.

He also expected that his grandparents would have plenty of
money to live on and all he'd need would be enough money from
the farm to pay the taxes and feed himself.

But now he would need to use some of his savings or possibly
all of it, and his grandparents might not have enough money to
support themselves.

His perspective had changed.

He still wanted the farm, still was trying to figure out a way to do
it, but...he definitely wasn't ready for a wife and children.

And that's kind of what he'd been thinking as he spent time with
Rose. He understood their dating had an endgame, and they had
agreed on one month, but he had been thinking that maybe he'd
be able to talk her into making it real.

Now, he couldn't think anything of the kind. He didn't have anything to offer her. Nothing but scratching out a living and maybe not even keeping the farm.

If he used all the money that he'd saved over the course of the years he'd been in The Cities to buy the farm, and if he couldn't make a go of it, he'd end up with nothing.

He couldn't ask a wife to go through that with him.

He wasn't sure how she would feel about children, but he couldn't ask her to hold off on them indefinitely.

They were already in their thirties. If it took ten years or more to make the farm profitable, they could lose their opportunity to ever have a family.

That seemed to be more than any woman should have to give up, and he wouldn't ask it of her. He knew how he felt when his wife had left him for a man who had kids, and they had children right away themselves when she hadn't wanted to have any with him.

It was a sensitive subject.

But by about two o'clock, he was thinking that maybe he should talk to Rose. Maybe there was something they could work out. Or... Maybe he just wanted to spend time with her, since she was so close and he'd been trying to avoid going to see her, which only made him think about her more.

Walking into the kitchen, he saw Rose pouring the last of a batch of raspberry jelly into a small half pint jar.

He'd forgotten that his grandma almost always made jelly out of the berries that they picked in the summer.

There was never enough time in the summer to do everything, so she just froze the berries, and then in the winter when things were slower, she strained the juice out of them and made them into jelly.

"Nice and warm in here," he said to the room in general.

Gram looked up at him, relief on her face.

He felt bad that he'd made her worry even for an instant. He'd tried to be clear when he left, he'd just been so...overwhelmed. Overwhelmed at his own lack of faith and their extreme living of their faith.

"I thought maybe you got lost out there?" Gram said.

"No. I just...got involved in fixing the fence and had some things I needed to think about too."

That was true. When he'd gotten out this morning, there'd been a cow out. He'd managed to get it back in okay and patched up the fence temporarily. But it had needed to be fixed, and he needed to think, and the two seemed to go hand in hand pretty well.

"Pap must be sleeping?"

"He is," Gram said, wiping her hands on the dishrag from the handle of the stove while Rose set the jelly pan in the sink and ran water into it.

She seemed quiet and subdued today as well.

That seemed odd, since she always had a smile and kind word.

"I... I'd like to talk to you guys, later. But right now, I need to head over to Mr. Blackstone's farm. His grain bin is still half full with pig feed. He said I could buy it from him, but I'd have to truck it myself. I figured I'd go over and get a load so I can feed the hog at the sale barn."

"Hog?" Gram said, tilting her head and looking confused.

"Oh. I guess in all the other excitement, I forgot to tell you. There was a sow that had piglets last night. Fifteen of them, and I made an impulse buy."

"That's not an impulse buy," Gram corrected him. "An impulse buy is a candy bar at the checkout counter. A sow?"

He laughed, possibly for the first time all day, looking at Rose's back. Odd that she almost seemed to be ignoring them.

Maybe she was just lost in thought.

"Rose?" he said, suddenly nervous. Had he done something to offend her? He thought back. They'd left on good terms at the sale. Sure, it had been cold and no one had lingered outside, but they'd had a good time, and she'd been smiling when she got in her car. He was sure of it.

She drained the water out of the pan, rinsing it before she set it upside down on the counter and turned.

"Hey. What?" she asked.

"I was wondering if you'd like to ride along with me?"

He hadn't been entirely sure he was going to ask, but as he recalled, she was only supposed to be here for a couple of hours to help over dinner and do any chores in the early afternoon. Thursday was a light day for her.

"Sure. All I have today is a date this evening with someone who probably won't care if I'm a little late getting ready," she said with a small smile, but she definitely did not seem to be her normal self.

"I don't want to take you early and leave Gram in the lurch, but I'm ready whenever you are."

"Gram said I was done when we were done with this. Is that still okay?" She looked at Gram.

"It sure is. The sun is out, and it's a beautiful day, even if it is still chilly. You youngsters go out and enjoy yourselves. I'm gonna go join Pap on the other easy chair and take a little nap. I feel like we've earned it with those pretty jars sitting there on the counter."

His gram seemed happy that Derek had asked Rose to go, although it concerned him that Rose seemed less thrilled.

Maybe it was whatever was bothering her.

If she wanted to get out of their agreement, he preferred that she tell him immediately.

And considering what he'd learned about the farm today, maybe that would be a good thing.

They didn't talk as they grabbed their coats and shoved their feet in their boots and walked out into the cold afternoon air.

"I brought the truck around, and I left it running so it would be warm."

"That's nice, although after working in the hot kitchen, I'm feeling pretty toasty," she said, her words light, her smile in place, but her internal spark, or whatever it was, just didn't seem quite right.

Still, he walked to her side of the truck and opened the door for her. She thanked him, climbing in without saying anything else.

He walked around and waited until they'd gotten on the road before he said anything.

"You're kind of quiet today. Is there something wrong?"

He figured the direct route was best. Although, part of him curled inside at the idea that this might be the last time they were together.

He'd just been thinking that very thing this morning though, with the farm. Thinking that this wasn't going to work. Whether it was now or whether it was later... Did it matter?

"It's nothing," she said, looking out the window at the flat, snow-covered North Dakota landscape.

"Nothing?"

She lifted a shoulder. "Yeah."

He didn't want to pry and almost let it go, but...maybe part of him didn't want to let go of the idea that there might be more between them.

That was true. But there was also part of him, a compassionate part, that saw another human being sitting beside him, someone who had something on her mind, and knew it was bothering her.

Maybe she was hurt. Maybe she'd gotten sad news. Maybe it was something else, but he just felt that as a friend, he should do his best to help her if he could.

So, he tried once more, when maybe, when he was younger, he wouldn't have. If she wouldn't answer, he'd have to let it go.

Hopefully this meant he was getting better at seeing people through Jesus's eyes and not through his own, much more selfish ones.

"You don't have to tell me if you don't want to. You just seem quiet, and a little withdrawn, and sad. I noticed it almost the second I walked into the kitchen. Again, you don't have to say anything, but...I did want to make sure that I didn't do anything to offend you."

"No. You didn't." She looked down at her lap, her fingers clasped together inside her gloves. Her thumbs catching back and forth on each other, and he supposed she was probably doing that without even really recognizing it.

"So it's something you can't talk about?" he prodded gently.

"I suppose maybe this would have something to do with the Dating Game. Because not everybody's pasts are all roses and cherries."

"Roses?" he asked, with a little grin, trying to get her to smile.

"Roses," she said, lifting her lips a little, then looking back down at her hands. "When I was growing up, I didn't want to be a doctor or a nurse or a teacher or any of the things that kids usually want to be. I just wanted to be a mom. That's it. I didn't even care if I was married for the longest time. You know, the way little kids are. I just wanted a baby to hold. I had a whole collection of doll babies, and I took care of them every day. It was really kind of pathetic." There was a little bit of humor in her tone, maybe laughing at her younger self.

He couldn't really relate at all. He'd never played with dolls, not once. He definitely never wanted to be a mom.

"I recall my sisters taking care of their dolls and crying if they had gotten dropped or stepped on. I can't say that I relate," he added, thinking she probably knew that.

"No. I didn't expect you to, I just... I just wanted you to know that my dream was to be a mom. I want kids. When I was old enough to babysit, I babysat every second I could. I didn't care if I got paid or not. It wasn't for the money. It was just because I love children. And I loved even the ones that other people thought were bad. I never thought they were bad. I... I just thought they needed love. Thought they needed to be guided in the right direction. And sure, maybe sometimes they needed to be disciplined, but I just love kids." She shrugged her shoulders, like words failed her, and she just couldn't figure out what more to say.

He wasn't sure what to say. Didn't know where she was coming from, where she was going with it. Didn't know how to draw more out of her.

"I've never seen you with children, but it sounds like you'd be really good with them," he finally said, not knowing what else to say.

"When I got married, I wanted to have children. Right away. I mean, that was the point. And before we were married, Harry acted like he was good with that. But once we were actually married, he wasn't interested. He wanted to wait. He said we needed to be established first, so we could take care of them properly."

Her lips pressed together, and her hands stopped moving and clasped together tightly.

"I didn't want to fight with him. We were young, we had time. So I went along with it. Then, of course, he left me for a woman who had children. Actually, she was pregnant when he walked out on me."

There was bitterness in her voice, anger. It wasn't hard to hear.

He thought of the unfairness of life and how sometimes the people who did everything right seemed to not come out on top, while the people who cheated, the people who hurt others in order to get ahead, the people who lied, the people who stepped on their friends and took advantage of them, just to make themselves look better, were the ones who often seemed to "win."

But that's where faith came in and the verse that he'd been thinking about earlier while working on the fence. *God is a rewarder of those who diligently seek Him.*

Just, sometimes, His rewards weren't rewards that a person expected or weren't earthly rewards.

But that was faith again, believing that whatever God gave would be better, would be worth it.

"Sometimes it's frustrating how unfair life is," he finally said, figuring she didn't want a lecture from him. He'd heard somewhere that women just wanted a shoulder to cry on, not advice.

He wasn't sure that was true all the time and maybe not even the wisest thing, but he didn't want her to clam up and quit talking when he started telling her how he thought she should live her life.

But it turned out he didn't have to. "I know that God says 'vengeance is mine.' That I shouldn't wish bad things on my ex. That the whole idea of us being together just to get him back was wrong." She looked over at him. "And I think we fixed that. I still need to apologize and admit that I lied, but I don't think that we're in this to try to get him back."

"No. You made the right decision there. I'm sure of it."

"And you helped," she said, and he appreciated her giving him credit.

Rose wasn't the type of person to not appreciate the people around her. He hoped he wasn't either.

"But that doesn't explain why you're so down today." And what was going on with her.

"No. I'm sorry. I'm actually happy," she said, but she seemed to put too much emphasis on being happy, like she was willing herself to be happy.

"Sounds like it," he said, not meaning to be sarcastic, but that's kind of the way it came out.

She sighed. "I know. And I feel terrible. This isn't something that I want my sister to find out, but Marigold, who just married Dodge this past summer, came to the house this morning with Dodge and announced that she was pregnant with twins." She continued on in a rush, like she didn't want to end there and have him come to the wrong conclusions. "And I'm so happy for her! She's thrilled. She's just glowing. She looks amazing, and Dodge is obviously proud and pleased, and they are going to make awesome parents."

She emphasized the word awesome, like she wanted to make sure that he knew that she loved her sister and had every faith that she was going to raise her children beautifully.

"But...it hurt me. Not my sister's actions, but I guess...God. That He would withhold this thing that I wanted all my life, longed for—didn't He give me that longing? Isn't that what He made a woman for? To have children. To love them, to nurture them, to bring them up in the nurture and admonition of the Lord. That's been my dream. Just a biblical wife and mom. That's it. And yet, God hasn't given it to me. But He gave it to my sister who, while she'll make a great mom, and I'm excited for her, she's never wanted children. I mean, I'm sure she wants the children she's carrying now, but this hasn't been a dream of hers!"

She laid her head back on the seat, her face raised toward the ceiling with her eyes closed. Almost in silent supplication to the Lord, asking him to right the wrong.

"I guess I'm thinking about Hannah."

"Oh, I can relate. I can so relate," she said without opening her eyes.

Now he got it. Her sister was happily married and pregnant. Not just pregnant but expecting twins. And she was getting what Rose had always longed for. It made the betrayal of her husband even worse. Since he'd left her for a woman with children and had three more after he'd left. When he wouldn't allow Rose to have any.

She'd wasted time with him, and now she was in another dead-end relationship.

And he just found out this morning he was hardly father material. Not with the farm in the condition it was.

Unless you don't buy the farm. You could do something else.

He hadn't considered that. Where did that thought come from anyway?

He had farming background, yes, but he also had a business background. Corporate background. He had a lot of skills he could put to use, doing pretty much anything. He could have a job in agriculture without actually living on a farm.

That was kind of putting the cart ahead of the horse. They hadn't even moved out of the fake relationship stage.

Not that there was such a stage for normal relationships.

He let out a breath, thinking that he had expected to have children too. His wife had done something very similar. But probably pointing that out wouldn't help anything. After all, he hadn't longed for children all his life like she had. He just kind of wanted them. It was a natural expectation when one got married, in his book anyway.

They'd made it out of Sweet Water and were driving west, far enough out that the Sweet Water mansion came into view.

He supposed it was kind of random, but he said, "Have you heard his story?" nodding his head toward the mansion when she looked at him.

"Ford Palmer?"

"Yeah."

"Yeah. I guess he's kind of a legend. I remember hearing about him in school."

"Yeah. He set pretty much all of the high school hockey records that still stand to this day."

"I know. It was always so unbelievable, because it was his brother who was the huge professional hockey star."

If she wondered where he was going with this, she didn't ask. She almost seemed relieved to not be talking about children and her sadness anymore.

"Yeah. And as successful as his brother was, Ford could have probably been even more so, except for the accident."

"Farming accidents happen. But it was sad that that ended his career before it even started. That's probably part of what made his story so poignant."

"Yeah, that and, you know, what happened afterward. About ten years or so, maybe a little longer, after his accident."

"I forget." She turned toward him, her eyes squinting like she was trying to remember, but her face was blank.

"He had a supermodel come to be his housekeeper slash personal assistant. He was scarred from the accident, lost fingers or something, his face was messed up. I've seen him around town, but when you talk to him, you kind of forget all that. Anyway, they fell in love, got married, and have children together."

Rose was silent for a moment; her eyes had gone from his face to staring out the window beside him. Unseeing. Like she was rolling what he'd said over in her mind, trying to make the connection he saw.

"It looked like he'd lost everything in high school with the accident."

"I think he thought that too. I heard he became a recluse for a while. Worked hard on his business and became a billionaire."

"From hockey star to recluse."

"He was a handsome fellow too, from what I hear. He must have felt like he lost everything."

"Like God took everything from him, after gifting him so greatly."

"Exactly. Why would God have gifted him with so much, just to take it all away?"

"That's a good question, and I guess the answer that's coming to my head is once you have it all and you lose it, you get something even better, and it makes you appreciate it because you realize how fleeting and what the true blessings are in life. The things that money can't buy."

"Right. But if he hadn't lost it, if he hadn't longed for what he had lost, longed for to the point where he hid himself away, maybe...maybe he wouldn't have appreciated true love when he found it. Maybe the idea of fortune and fame would have ruined him. But as it is, he's a godly man who loves his wife and has been faithful to her since before they were married. They have beautiful children, who are growing up to serve the Lord. He's got everything."

She seemed to understand when he said that Ford had everything, he wasn't talking about the mansion they'd passed or the money he had. He was talking about his wife and children. "It's hard for me to imagine that I could need to learn to appreciate a child more, but I can appreciate the fact that if God ever gives me one, I'll not want to take advantage of that."

"But you know how to relate to people who long for children now. Because you've been there. You know how to relate to people who see others getting exactly what they want and have to deal with the jealousy and the idea that God isn't blessing you and maybe He doesn't love you."

Her eyes opened wide and shot to his face, like she was astounded at his astuteness.

He really hadn't been sure where those words came from. Just... It seemed like when God didn't give a person what they wanted, it meant He didn't love you.

"But parents keep things from their children because they know it's good for them. And it's because they love them that they don't give them what they want, not the other way around."

"That's a really hard pill for me to swallow, because I can't imagine that God would think it's somehow good for me to not have kids of my own."

"Sometimes we can't see the reason until we look back. That's where faith comes in, to enable us to look ahead and know that God's reasons are right, and good, and just, and the very best for us, even if we can't see it."

The truck motor droned on, broken by the cracks in the pavement as they flew over them, the blue sky cloudless and brilliant, the flat landscape stretching on and on.

The silence in the cab stretched out along with it, and he thought maybe their conversation was over. Maybe he'd stepped on her toes a little too much, and she just wanted to be away from him.

"I feel like it's right there. Like I'm almost to the point where I can say okay, God, this must be the best thing for me, and if I never have children, I'll just assume that You want me to understand that You know best." She shook her head and huffed out a breath. "I'm almost to that point," she said, emphasizing the *almost*.

"Wouldn't it be nice if we could just snap our fingers and make our feelings follow what we know to be right? Even if you can get your thoughts right, sometimes it's really hard to get those feelings to turn around."

"That's coming from a man, who isn't supposed to have problems with that. I think it's one hundred times harder for a woman."

"You might be right. Although maybe men just have different feelings to corral. Since we seem to have more trouble with anger, and impatience, and arrogance. Lust. Maybe just because those are manly feelings that we're allowed to show."

"Maybe," she said, and for the first time, she smiled a true smile. Maybe it wasn't quite as bright as her normal ones, but it reached her eyes as she took him in. "Thank you. I guess maybe I just needed to talk it out a little. I still feel a little envious, but the jealousy is gone. And I feel like I might—at some point—be able to be content, even if God never gives me what I want. I'm just going to assume that He's going to give me something better. I'm going to set my heart on that."

"That's a good idea. And a nice thought to think."

"Thanks for helping me get there."

Chapter 12

My hubby would say say "yes dear" to wife, but kidding aside,
never go to bed angry.
- Cyndi Newlan from Ohio

They picked up the feed at Mr. Blackburn's farm, and Derek had wanted to stop at the auction barn and feed his sow and check on the piglets.

Coleman had said he'd keep an eye on them, and Rose knew that they would be well taken care of, but a farmer's job was to take care of his animals and crops. Derek had that instinct.

She loved the auction barn, and who wouldn't want to see the piglets, so she didn't mind at all.

Plus, she'd been having a good time with Derek. Somehow he managed to talk her out of her depression-like mood and remind her that there were things that were more important than what she wanted. And just because she wanted it didn't mean that God needed to give it to her. That He was God for a reason, and she wasn't.

Somehow Derek had managed to say all that to her without really saying anything.

He hadn't made her feel bad or made her feel guilty for being jealous, even though he could have.

Grabbing the bucket of feed that he'd filled for that purpose, Derek hefted it out of his pickup and looked at her. "Ready?"

She nodded, and he held his hand out, just stretched it out to her, and she looked at it.

Did he mean for her to take it?

She supposed there would be this awkwardness even if their relationship was real, but she had a tendency to second-guess everything. Wondering whether he meant it or how exactly they needed to proceed, having never had a fake relationship to know what to do in one.

Deciding if he didn't want to hold her hand, he could pull it away, she grabbed it and laced her fingers with his, glad the pickup had been warm enough that she finally pulled off her gloves.

His smile seemed genuine, and it almost felt like he wasn't doing it for show.

Deciding she needed to stop dissecting every move they made in the relationship and just let things go, she returned his grin as they walked toward the bottom end of the pen area to go in the back way.

Derek let go of her hand to open the door for her, and she ducked in.

As a child, she'd always loved running around the different aisles, feeling like the whole auction barn was such a maze and yet one she knew like the back of her hand.

Now, it just felt comforting, the smell, the sounds, and even when empty, the memories lingered.

"Oh, they're sleeping!" she said, automatically lowering her voice.

The sow had lifted her head when they'd stopped at the fence, but she lay back down when she decided they weren't a threat.

All the babies were cuddled up to her, seeking her warmth.

They stood there admiring them for a little bit in silence, just watching how the babies jerked in their sleep, and their little bodies moved up and down with each slumbering breath.

It wouldn't take much to make them a massive squirming wakeness, with little pink bodies going everywhere, and that would be fun to watch as well.

There was just something about baby animals that was fascinating.

"I'll go grab some water," she said.

"No. I'll do it. I saw a hose last night, down at the end of this aisle. Is that the closest one?"

"Yeah. And there should be a bucket in the room right beside it. There's a door there."

He nodded, leaving the bucket of feed and walking down the aisle.

Footsteps above her caused her to look up. The sow snorted, lifting her head as well.

"Hey," Coleman said from above her. "I thought I heard the door open."

"Yeah. It's just Derek and me. He came to feed his sow."

"So... I haven't quite figured out what's going on with you two. Do you really like him?"

Normally, Coleman didn't butt into her business at all. He left the whole relationship thing alone. Other than being a protective big brother and occasionally posturing to protect them, especially if he felt like someone who didn't deserve them was interested, he didn't get into the emotional side.

Maybe having all the sisters had made him leery, she wasn't sure.

Of course, he had something in his past as well. Something she had never had enough nerve to ask about, although Lavender had, and he'd shut her down immediately and not very nicely.

Normally Coleman was extremely kind to his sisters, benevolent almost, but he hadn't allowed her to do more than ask about the ring that he wore around his neck before he'd told her it was none of her business.

Lavender was not an easy person to discourage, but she never asked about it again, and while Rose was definitely curious about the small ring that lay against his chest on a chain, she wouldn't ask either.

She supposed everyone was entitled to secrets. Coleman maybe more than some, because of the heavy load that had been placed on his shoulders at a young age.

Still, she didn't hold it against him, and she answered his questions as honestly as she could.

"I do. He's a good man."

"But you're just faking it?" he asked, like he really wanted to know the answer to the question.

"Sometimes I forget that I am. I guess that doesn't make sense."

"No. It doesn't make sense, and it's probably not very smart." He said the words thoughtfully.

"I know. I get that, but normally I would just say forget it." She'd been tempted to. "But I'm not sure what it is about it, but it...feels right."

She knew he wouldn't understand the whole feels thing. He didn't put much stock in feelings, and he'd probably give her a hard time for doing so.

It wasn't her emotions. It was in her heart where it didn't feel right. She wasn't sure she could explain the difference to Coleman, or if he'd ever even understand.

Looking down the aisle, she could see that Derek had the bucket full and was shutting off the hose.

Coleman's eyes followed her glance, over the railing of the catwalk he stood on. "I was just checking it out with you. I want to offer him a business deal, but I wasn't sure how you fit into things, and...if there's going to be a big nasty breakup, with lots of hurt feelings and drama, I'd rather stay out."

"No. Please, don't not offer him something because of me. Really. He's...not that kind of man. Whatever happens, he's not going to treat me wrong."

She was as assured of that as the day was long. She knew she could trust him, trust him to do right by her. No matter what.

Maybe because of the way he treated his grandparents. Maybe because of the way he talked to her in the truck. Or maybe it was just an intuition that she had.

But she knew it.

Coleman stared at her, his eyes boring into her, the way only an older brother's could. Finally, as Derek started down the aisle toward her after putting the hose away, he said, "Okay. I think it can be very beneficial to him, and I know he could use a little boost up because of him wanting to buy the farm and get started. That's not easy, and I think I have something that will help him." He straightened from leaning against the railing. "I'll be right down."

Rose couldn't explain the excited twirling of her heart. Other than to say that if something good happened to Derek, of course she'd be happy. She wanted to see him succeed. He was a nice man.

He was more than a nice man.

She could admit to herself that she believed that. But she wasn't sure what to do with it. She felt like she was stuck in limbo.

Maybe she just had to wait and see what the Lord did. Just live each day as it came and not try to figure everything out before she was meant to know it.

The thought was scary yet comforting at the same time.

"She's still sleeping?" Derek said as he came back with the water.

"Yeah," Rose said, her hand on the top rail of the board fence. "If you need me to, I can open the gate."

"No. I think I can reach the trough, just dump it in from here. No point in risking losing a little one out the opening and having Mama get upset when it starts squealing."

"Oh, you've experienced that?" She grinned.

"Yes. And that marks you, long after you are finally safe."

"Yeah. I know exactly what you mean." They shared smiles, and she was able to read the humor in his eyes and also the healthy respect he had for a mama protecting her babies.

He dumped the feed in the trough, and the sow snorted, lifting her head, sniffing with more snorts, then lumbering to her feet, the babies who had been sleeping on top of her and between her legs flopping everywhere.

Rose watched with some concern as she walked amongst her scrambling little ones to get to the trough.

It seemed like a miracle that she didn't step on anyone.

Derek poured the water in, wetting the feed, and the sow stuck her nose down in, snorting happily, munching greedily.

"I was trying to count them, to make sure we didn't lose any more, but it's impossible with the way they're moving all around."

"It was hard to count them yesterday while she was having them. I said fourteen, not counting the dead one, and I was ninety per-cent confident." Coleman walked over to the fence, leaning his forearms on the top board beside Derek's. "I guess I should have said that when I gave you the numbers."

"It's not going to make a difference. Plus, we could lose a couple before it's all said and done."

"You sure could. I wish we were set up to put a heat lamp in and let the babies lie under that, kind of like a farrowing pen."

"I know you lose less babies that way, and that's better for the bottom line, but I kinda like the idea of them being with their mom the way they're supposed to be. Even if that does mean more risk for the babies."

"Yeah. Natural is best, but really, pigs weren't necessarily meant to look exactly like that. They're definitely bred to be bigger in the hams and wider through the middle for more bacon, which makes raising little ones harder."

"I agree."

Rose stayed silent, liking the fact that Derek wanted to go with a more natural approach. That seemed better to her as well. Although Coleman was right that a normal pig didn't have that issue because of genetics.

Still, she kept her mouth closed, because she was curious as to what Coleman was going to offer Derek. Although, maybe she should excuse herself to give them privacy.

She opened her mouth to do that very thing, when Coleman said, "You have a couple minutes? I want to talk to you about something."

Derek shrugged beside her and shifted, setting the bucket down and leaning his own forearms on the top of the board fence. "I have a hot date tonight, but I think she'll understand if I'm a little late." He echoed her words of earlier, which made her grin.

Coleman didn't seem to get the joke, or maybe he was thinking about what he wanted to say. Whatever it was, he didn't laugh.

After a moment or two of silence, he said, "I have a contact, one of those guys with more money than brains, if you know what I mean." Coleman looked serious.

Derek nodded. "I've met a few of those guys, worked with some of them. It's not always pleasant."

"Exactly. Sometimes they're a little...hard to deal with." He paused for a moment, as though he was going to say more, but then he didn't. "This fella, John Maxwell, contacted me a couple of days ago asking if I knew of any farms in the area who might be interested in getting into buffalo."

"Buffalo?"

"Yeah. Apparently he's got some restaurants of his own, and that's one of the specialties they serve. I guess folks in the city pay a lot of money for it. It is supposed to be healthy for you but only if you grass-finish them."

Derek grunted, like he'd been up on that, knew what Coleman was saying.

Rose was relieved when they didn't go into a tangent about grass fed versus corn finished. She wanted to find out what Coleman was offering.

"He's looking for a place that will raise his buffalo exclusively. He wants them finished a certain way, wants them aged a certain way, and he wants them killed and butchered on the farm. That will be the kicker. You'll need to put in a butchering shop on your property."

"I see."

"The rates he quoted me are more than worth it. If you have the capital upfront to put in the shop, and you have the farm, this could end up being a profitable business."

"What about the stock? I have no idea where to buy buffalo or what constitutes good genetics, and I can imagine they're pricy."

"He actually has a herd. He's been paying to have them grown and finished. The guy that's been doing it is getting out. I think he's retiring to an island in Jamaica, from what John said." Coleman did grin a little at that.

Derek huffed a laugh. "That guy's got more brains than money?"

"That's exactly what I was thinking. If I had any brains, that's where I'd be. Especially this time of year."

Rose heard him talking, but she knew neither one of them meant it. Both of them loved North Dakota, and while winter did drag on and sometimes seemed never ending, neither one of them would want to be in Jamaica. She knew for a fact that Coleman wouldn't be able to sit still for more than a day, and he'd be swimming off the island by the end of the week if he couldn't find anyone to take him off.

He'd prefer swimming with sharks to doing nothing.

"John is looking for someone to take over, since that other fella's retiring. His kids aren't interested in taking the farm, and they're selling it. So John needs a place to take his herd of buffalo."

"How many are there?"

"He has about three hundred head. He uses about one a day between his restaurants, so give or take. He told me he'd like to work the herd up to four hundred or so, because he wants to open another joint, but that's still in the works. You have time."

"I see. I would have to look into it. I don't really know much about buffalo."

"Neither do I, but John said that the fellow who's retiring would be willing to talk to you or whoever takes over about it. If someone's willing. I just know that the money that he quoted me was crazy amounts, and you'd almost have to be blundering stupid in order to not make money."

"Well, I hope that doesn't describe me, but sometimes it probably does."

Coleman laughed, and Rose smiled. She supposed everyone could be blundering stupid at times.

"If you're interested, let me know," Coleman said, straightening, clapping Derek on the shoulder. "John is eager to get his herd moved before spring, since calving will start in April."

"I see. How far away are they right now?"

"About fifty miles south," Coleman said right away.

"All right. I'll be in touch. I want to think about it a little. Talk to my grandparents." Derek straightened too, and almost without seeming to think about it, he put his arm around her shoulders, not holding her tight necessarily, just holding her.

She found she liked it, other than the odd look that Coleman gave them.

Odd in that he just seemed like he couldn't quite figure out exactly what was going on, and it bothered him.

But he didn't say anything, just shook hands with Derek and said he had to get back to work.

As he was walking away, Derek looked back at the sow, who was still eating happily, her babies heaped up in a pile in the spot where she'd been lying down.

"Looks like they're all alive at least, and she's eating well. Did you see anything that struck you as something we need to check out?"

She assumed he was wondering if all the babies were eating, and that's what she had been looking for as she'd watched them squirm and wiggle and readjust themselves into a heap.

None of them seemed overly skinny, but it was definitely something they were going to need to watch.

"I thought they all looked good, but maybe we can stop in tonight?"

"If you don't mind. That's not exactly date material, but I suppose if you insist." He looked at her and winked.

She laughed outright. "I'm sorry to disappoint you, but I'm never going to be a fancy girl." She shook her head.

"I had one of those. Never again."

While his words didn't exactly make her happy, because it obviously hurt him to think that it hadn't worked out, she was pretty sure that he didn't pine after his ex.

Which was a relief.

She'd already had one person cheat on her; that was something she didn't want to have happen again.

Chapter 13

*Pray for your spouse even through the good times as that will
get you through the tough times.
- Sharon W Steward from Ontario, Canada*

"Come on in! I don't think Rose is quite ready yet. But I'll holler up the stairs and see if she is," Mrs. Baldwin said as she held the door open for Derek to step through.

"You don't need to do that. We're not in any rush."

"If I don't, she might be up there forever, talking to her sisters and letting them change her clothes yet again."

"That bad?"

"It's normal." Mrs. Baldwin shook her head, her kind and intelligent eyes sparkling. "Her sisters and I are headed out, so at the very least they won't be in her hair anymore, and she can finally settle on something."

He wasn't sure exactly what that meant. Although he supposed after being married, he knew that women had a tendency to change their minds three or four times before they settled on the outfit they truly wanted to wear. Or before they settled back on the first outfit that they tried on to begin with.

It was something he'd never figured out but he'd learned to live with. Figuring that if she said she'd be ready at seven, he might as well plan on eight. And they might get out the door a little bit early.

But checking his phone, he saw that he was actually early and figured he might as well settle in to wait.

He'd no longer thought that than steps on the stairs made him turn.

He wasn't sure what he'd been expecting—a ball gown from the way Mrs. Baldwin was talking—but Rose ran downstairs in jeans and a loose sweater, with boots that were maybe a little more stylish than sensible but still looked warm.

"You look nice," he said, thinking that beautiful was more descriptive than nice, but he didn't want her to think that he wasn't sincere. Or that he was just flattering her.

Although, it was the truth.

Her cheeks were bright, and maybe she had some makeup on her eyes, he wasn't sure how to tell, but she looked a little different than what she normally did, but that might be because her hair was down.

He didn't think he'd seen it down before, and it flowed in waves over her shoulders, almost down to her waist.

That alone made his breath catch.

But with the bright blue eyes and an unaffected, happy smile, he figured he was going to have a hard time not staring at his date tonight.

"You never said where we were going, and I couldn't figure out whether I should wear something dressy or not, but I can change if I need to," Rose said, her hands smoothing down her jeans.

"You're fine. I hadn't made any choices about where we're going to go. Figured we'd decide together."

"Oh?" She raised her brows.

"No. We hadn't really talked about it, and I didn't want to take you somewhere you didn't want to go. I was thinking about ice-skating."

"That sounds like fun," Rose said, sounding like she meant it. "Oh! I left my purse upstairs. I'll be right back." She spun on her toe and ran up the stairs.

He brushed his hands down his jeans, wondering if he'd remembered to put on clean socks. He couldn't recall. He hadn't brought his skates, either. But she kind of looked like she expected him to know where they were going. If it had been a real date, he probably would have.

As it was, he'd been torn between thinking about her and wanting her to like him, and not in a fake date kind of way.

Knowing him and his inability to be a brilliant conversationalist, he probably would spend the evening talking about buffalo.

Just then the doorbell rang, and Mrs. Baldwin called out from somewhere in the kitchen, "Mind getting that?"

"Sure," he said, turning and looking at the door.

It must not be someone who was here often, since they were using the doorbell and not knocking on their way in.

The Baldwin household was just as casual as his always had been growing up.

"Hey," he said as he opened the door to a woman that he didn't recognize, with what looked like a three- or four-year-old kid on her hip. A girl, if the pink hat was any indication. Although he couldn't see any hair coming out from underneath her hat, and the clothes were bulky, designed for warmth and not style.

"Hey, is Rose here?" the woman said, her brows squeezing together, like she wasn't sure she was at the right house.

"Sure. Come on in. She's upstairs, but she's coming right back down." He didn't have the door shut before he heard Rose behind him, saying, "Becky! And Naomi! So good to see you. Looks like you got a new blankie," she said, in a bit of a babyish voice but enunciating each word clearly.

The little girl smiled at her and quit clinging to her mother, leaning over and holding her arms out.

"Oh my goodness! I'm happy to see you too!" Rose said, dropping her purse on the floor and taking the little girl easily, giving her a hug, and planting a kiss on the top of her head.

"Oh thank goodness," Becky said, sounding truly relieved.

"What's the matter?" Rose asked, her head still snuggled up next to Naomi's.

"She wouldn't stay at the sitter's. It's been a while since she's been there, but she screamed and would not let go of me. I am late." She looked at her watch, a fancy thing with a huge face and a delicate strap. And that's when Derek realized that she was dressed much fancier than Rose was. Like maybe she was going out too. "I'm supposed to be meeting someone for supper. A date. I've only been with him once, and I don't know him that well, and I don't want to drag Naomi along with me. Since she wouldn't stay at my normal sitter's... I know you never have anything going on, so I was hoping that you—" she said, practically blinking her eyes as her lips pouted, pleading on her face.

Derek could see the conflict moving across Rose's face.

"Um... Becky, I was actually going out myself, and I would say that one of my sisters would watch her, but my mom and they are going to look at a herd of cattle that a farmer over the way is thinking about running through the auction barn. They have papers, and Mom wanted to get an eyeball on them to make sure that they're what he says they are." Rose seemed to cut herself off, realizing she was rambling.

Derek figured he knew why.

If they hadn't talked in the truck today, he would have been clueless, but he thought he understood what was going on.

Rose wasn't necessarily conflicted because she couldn't tell her friend, or acquaintance, no. She was more reluctant because she didn't want to let go of Naomi. And with the way Naomi had her little arms wrapped around Rose's neck, Naomi didn't want anyone else.

Knowing how Rose had longed for a child and how she loved children, Derek couldn't stand there without saying anything. He figured that Rose wouldn't want to cancel her date with him, since obviously, they'd been planning that much longer than Becky's spur-of-the-moment request.

"Rose?" he said, kind of low, knowing that they wouldn't be able to have a private conversation right in front of Becky but wanting to offer somehow. "I remember what you said in the truck today. This is your call."

"Is this your date?" Becky asked, wiggling her eyebrows and giving Derek a look that made him slightly uncomfortable.

"I'm sorry. Derek, this is Becky Briggs, she lives down the road from us. Moved in a few months ago. I've watched Naomi for her several times and loved it."

"And Naomi loves you. I think the kicker was the last time you watched her, you took her to the sale barn, and that's all she talked about for weeks afterward."

"I think we had baby ducks that time. We don't usually have those, and they came through the barn instead of the little shed outside, which was closed for the winter."

"Whatever it was, she was enchanted." Becky shook her head and held out her hand, bracelets rattling on her wrist, her long nails sparkling pink in the light. "Nice to meet you, Derek," she said, looking at him slightly under her lashes and blinking her eyes a couple of times.

He gripped her hand, feeling a little awkward, because she seemed so...fancy. He'd worked with women like this a good bit, but she just seemed a little out of place here in North Dakota.

Maybe she'd brighten the place up some.

She was the kind of high-maintenance woman that he had sworn he wasn't going to have anything to do with again.

But she was on her way to a date with another man. It seemed odd that she'd be looking at him and wiggling her brows, and...flirting? That's what it seemed like she was doing.

He wasn't the slightest bit interested in someone who couldn't keep her eyes on one man at a time.

He'd already been with someone like that.

Plus, seeing her beside Rose made Rose look classy and elegant. Refined. While Becky seemed overdone and fake.

Two things he knew Rose wasn't. Two things he didn't want to have in someone he was with.

He didn't need to compare the two though. Becky held no interest for him. No matter what she was doing with her eyes. Maybe she had something stuck in them.

"Are you sure you don't mind?" Rose asked, biting her lip. Obviously wanting to spend time with the little girl but not wanting to hurt his feelings.

He found his feelings weren't hurt. Maybe he would have been a little bit put out if he hadn't talked to her earlier.

"I'm sure." He could find something to do. He didn't have to go on a date tonight.

"Can I talk to you for a moment?" Rose asked, indicating the living room. Apparently she wanted privacy.

"Sure," he said, glancing at Becky and saying, "Excuse us," before following Rose into the living room.

She turned as soon as she stepped inside and waited for him to stop in front of her, shifting Naomi who seemed to have no intention of getting down.

"I want to spend the evening with you. Fake dating aside, I...I like you, and I was really looking forward to this."

"Okay. That's easy. We'll just do something with Naomi." His eyes fell on the little girl who was looking at him from underneath Rose's chin where she had her head tucked.

"Have you eaten yet? Would you like some pancakes?" he asked, figuring people usually had the ingredients to make pancakes at least. And if not, surely they could find some somewhere. Even if they had to make a trip to the grocery store.

She nodded her head without lifting it from Rose's shoulder.

"Maybe we can go see the mother sow and her piglets," he suggested, lifting his brows at Rose.

Her eyes lit up, and he assumed she thought that was a great idea.

His eyes shifted down to Naomi, who looked interested, but maybe she didn't know what a sow was. Or what did he know? Maybe pigs weren't her thing.

"She loves the auction barn. She was there the last time and just had such a great time. You heard Becky."

He smiled, and his heart did something weird. Just seeing Rose standing there holding the little girl, looking so happy, natural, maternal.

Funny, he couldn't imagine wanting to go on a date and bring a child along. Never in his life had he ever considered thinking that was a good idea, but...with Rose, his thinking had shifted some.

Maybe, just maybe, he had taken the high road with his ex, and God might actually be turning that miserable situation into something that...he never considered could be possible.

"Are you sure?" she asked, looking up at him.

"Let's go tell her. I think this will be more fun than anything else we could have done anyway." And somehow, he thought maybe that might be true.

They walked back out. Naomi gripped Rose's neck tighter, like she was afraid that Rose was going to hand her back over to her mother.

That seemed odd, that a child that young would want someone other than their mom, but Rose seemed to have that way about her. And he supposed that if he spent any time around her, he might find out that that was the way kids normally were when she was around.

"We'll do it," Rose announced, like Becky had just given her the greatest gift in the world.

"Fantastic. Thank you so much. I hope you don't mind if I run. I'll grab her overnight bag and just set it right here inside the door, okay?"

That made Derek blink.

Overnight bag?

But Rose didn't seem to turn a hair. "That's fine. I think maybe we'll go in the kitchen and see if we can find the ingredients for pancakes."

"Oh, thanks. I hadn't fed her supper yet."

Derek didn't say anything but followed Rose into the kitchen where Mrs. Baldwin had disappeared, maybe going up the back stairs, he wasn't sure.

"So do you think you can say hi to Mr. Derek?" Rose said to Naomi as she set her down on the counter. Naomi seemed to go reluctantly, clutching her blanket, her hand still trying to grip Rose's shoulders.

"Do you want me to hold you? Or do you want to make pancakes?"

"Hold me," Naomi said.

"How about you sit, and I'll look for the ingredients for the pancakes," Derek suggested.

"Okay. If you don't mind. I can tell you where they are. Maybe once Naomi sees you starting to make them, she'll want to stand and help."

"That's what I was figuring," he said.

She had just directed him to the second cupboard door from the right when her sisters came down the stairs.

Just a few seconds later and they were in the kitchen.

"Was that Becky at the door?" Glory asked. He could recognize her. The twins he wasn't too sure about.

"It was. She left us a gift." Rose scrunched down and rubbed her nose with Naomi's. Which made Naomi laugh while she rubbed her nose against Rose's.

"She takes advantage of you," one of the other girls said.

"She gives me a gift to watch. It makes me happy. And maybe I get to be a little bit of a blessing to Naomi."

Derek figured she was probably more of a blessing to Becky, although maybe not in the way she wanted to be.

But a person never knew how their influence was going to rub off, and maybe eventually she would influence Becky for good.

Neither of the girls said anything else before their mom came into the kitchen.

"I'm sorry I didn't stop and say hi, I was reaching for the canister that we keep on top of the cupboards, and my shirt ripped. I had to run upstairs, and I went the back way."

"I wondered where you disappeared to," Rose said, grinning at her mom, while the girls laughed at the idea of their mom breaking out of her shirt.

"So, you're like the Incredible Hulk?" Glory said, bumping shoulders with her mom.

"You've lived with me all these years and didn't know it?" her mom joked back, not missing a beat.

It was funny that he felt oddly out of place but strangely comfortable in the kitchen with all the ladies present joking and talking.

They chatted like he wasn't there, no one treating him specially, which made him feel comfortable, but it was so unusual.

Finally, the girls and their mom headed out the door, and it was strangely quiet.

"Do you want to help?" Rose asked Naomi in the now silent kitchen.

Naomi nodded. Rose stood up, going to the refrigerator and pulling out the eggs. "You look a little uncomfortable there. I know you had a sister." She set the eggs down on the counter.

Maybe these were Dating Game questions, but regardless, but he didn't really think so. He felt like Rose was truly interested in him.

"I had an older sister and older brother and a younger sister and younger brother. So I was right smack dab in the middle."

"Wow. Sometimes that's an awkward place to be."

"Yeah. There were definitely times where I wished I had less siblings. And... We didn't get along like that."

"A lot of families don't. It seems like we're all torn in different directions now, and you have to deliberately keep your family together, or everybody has their own thing that they do."

"Insightful. And probably something most parents don't realize until their kids aren't interested in being a family anymore." He looked at Naomi, thinking of Becky running off, assuming that she was going to be staying overnight, whether it was with her date or without, maybe she just figured she'd be back late and didn't want to pick her daughter up. But... He thought that maybe she should put her daughter first.

But that was judgmental, and he probably shouldn't think those things until he'd walked a mile in her shoes. Which he really didn't want to do.

He wasn't interested in the dating game anyway. The real-life dating game. Where dating was a game.

"So your parents moved south, leaving your grandparents here. Where are the rest of your siblings?"

"Scattered all over the place. I have one in Maine, one in South Carolina. Two in Texas. My parents are in Arizona."

"Wow. They really are scattered."

"Yeah. I guess maybe that makes me all the more determined to come back here and put roots down."

"Do you mind if I ask about the buffalo thing? What you thought? I don't want to be nosy if you don't want to talk to me about it."

He had been afraid that was all he'd think to talk about, and here, she'd brought it up. "It might help to talk it out. I'll need to talk to my grandparents, and I didn't get to do that when I was home, since I wanted to get the feeding done so I could come out here."

Her lips tightened a little, and a look that he almost would term guilt passed over her face.

"I'm not sure what that look meant, but if you're feeling bad that I thought I was going on a date and we ended up here in the kitchen making pancakes with a cute little girl, don't be. I... I grew out of the whole needing to go on a date to be entertained thing a long time ago." And that was no joke. He really would rather stay home. And just be with the people he loved.

"How did you read that on my face?" she asked, looking up at him with a bemused expression.

"Well, I'd say it's because I have sisters, but that's not true. I guess, I guess when you care about someone, you watch them."

Maybe he shouldn't have said that. Because he wasn't sure exactly where they were in their relationship.

She had been helping Naomi hold an egg in her hand, showing her how to tap it against the edge of the counter, as the little girl stood on a chair that Rose had pulled over.

But she stopped, her hands on Naomi's, her eyes on him.

"Really?" she asked, as though that would be hard to believe.

"Yeah," he said. He didn't know what was going to happen with the farm, with the money, with the buffalo. But maybe, instead of worrying about having everything in a row first, he'd just consider himself blessed if he found someone who would stand beside him for the rest of his life.

Chapter 14

Two things: 1. Letting your spouse be who he is. Not trying to change him. Celebrating the things that interest him, even when they are not interesting to me. 2. Providing honest and loving feedback. When he does something that hurts my feelings, it's important to tell him, not bottle it up. I wait until I can tell him without being hurtful in return.
– Sarah from FL

"Is she asleep?" Derek asked as Rose stirred on the couch, careful not to jiggle Naomi, who was snuggled up, asleep, on her lap.

After they'd made pancakes, they'd gone to the sale barn, where Naomi had spent more than an hour watching the sow and her piglets.

They'd gone home. Rose had given her a bath, and they played some games in the living room before Naomi had climbed up on Rose's lap and settled down. Derek and she had whispered softly, talking about the feasibility of raising buffalo, with Derek wondering if he would be able to put a slaughterhouse in or at least a small butcher shop and figure out how to run it.

They'd done a little bit of research online, and Rose had told him that she knew an older couple who had a small butcher shop north of Sweetwater. She'd get in touch with them tomorrow, and maybe they'd be able to pay them a visit. Derek had seemed pretty excited about the idea.

All in all, it had been a wonderful "date" even though it had been different than any date she'd ever heard of.

Derek had been so good to her and even better to Naomi. He'd rolled with their changes and hadn't seemed put out at all.

Maybe that was the way a lot of men were, but she'd never heard about anyone like that. She tried to imagine Coleman spending a happy evening on the couch with a woman and a child instead of going on a date. She wasn't sure whether that would go over or not.

Her brother was really all she had to base things on, other than her ex, who got angry if things didn't go the way he wanted.

Derek had been the furthest thing from angry all evening.

"She didn't wake up, and I think I should be able to put her in bed."

"I'll carry her," he offered softly.

She had spent most of the evening smiling, and at his comment, her lips tilted up again. His consideration was endearing. He always seemed to be thinking about what she might want or what he could do to help her, and he wasn't afraid to offer or jump in. Like at the auction barn.

Like tonight.

She knew her eyes were soft and her smile admiring, but she couldn't help it. He'd been the perfect date, even if they hadn't been *on* the perfect date.

His arm slid under the sleeping girl, and Naomi stirred softly, her hands gripping tighter around her blankie, her mouth working around the thumb she had stuck in it.

His hand brushed Rose's upper arm, but she kept her eyes on Naomi, trying to be gentle and move slowly so the little girl didn't wake.

She'd clung to Rose all evening and hadn't asked for her mother once, but a lot of times when children were sleeping or around bedtime, they would want the security of their parents or their own bed.

That was part of the reason Rose hadn't tried to put her to bed but had sat on the couch talking and cuddling until she fell asleep.

They were able to hand off the little girl without her waking, and Derek cradled her close to his chest.

Rose knew she should look away, because seeing him with the little one made her heart do funny things in her chest.

She turned and went up the steps before him, leading him to her room where she had a daybed set up, since this wasn't the first time that Becky had dropped Naomi off and given her an overnight bag.

Sometimes overnight turned into three or four days. It was not uncommon for that to happen. Worse, it was even normal for Becky to not call, not check, not even wonder what her child was doing.

That was part of the reason Rose's sisters told her that she was allowing Becky to take advantage of her, but she didn't care.

She loved Naomi and would take her anytime Becky didn't want her. For as long as Becky would allow her to. And she would do the very best she could to provide a stable influence and lots of love and care to the little girl. After all, what would it be like to have a mom who would just drop you off and never even ask about you for days?

Rose couldn't imagine, and she wanted to do everything in her power to let Naomi know that she loved her.

Derek followed her into the room, and she didn't turn the light on, allowing the light from the bathroom down the hall to shine in through the door.

"Watch the edge of the bed here," she said as they navigated around the sharp corner of her bed to the small daybed on the other side. "This is where she sleeps." She pulled the blankets down and adjusted the pillow, then stepped back as Derek bent over carefully and gently laid the little girl onto the bed.

He reached for the covers, but Rose had already been moving them up. Their hands brushed.

Rose bit her lip but didn't look at him.

She worked around tough men. Guys who were capable, men who could fix equipment, take care of any problem, do wiring and plumbing, deliver a calf in the field, in the dead of winter, in below-zero temperatures.

Who could do anything—solve problems, take care of themselves and their families, take physical hits, financial hits, weather hits, and still keep on working. But none of those men did anything to her heart the way seeing Derek did as she watched how gentle and careful he was with Naomi.

She couldn't look at him. She'd never felt like this before, not like her heart had so much...something... in it, and it could barely fit in her chest.

She wanted to reach over and touch him, to stand beside him looking down at the child like she was theirs.

That was just too weird.

Little Naomi, who had turned on her side as soon as he laid her down, pulled her blankie closer to her, tucking her hand under her chin without ever opening her eyes.

Derek straightened beside her, and they stood looking down at the little one.

Rose could stand there all night, just watching her breathe, seeing the sweet little dip of her nose and the peaceful relaxation of her face.

Just loving watching her.

But the feeling she had that made the inside of her chest riot made her restless, and she felt like she needed to go. To walk. To move. To get away. She couldn't do this.

Derek had been forced into proximity with her, and the very least she could do for him would be to not fall in love with him.

Moving to go, she wasn't paying attention and took two steps before bumping her leg into the corner of her bed.

Pain shot down to her toes and up to her hip, but she closed her mouth over the sound that wanted to come out, unwilling to wake Naomi.

She still turned, checking to see if the muted thump had made the child stir.

"She didn't move," Derek said.

She nodded, moving the rest of the way out of the room, trying not to limp. She held her hand on the door, waiting for Derek to go through so she could close it softly.

Focusing on not feeling his heat or smelling his scent that reminded her of character and care and consideration. Something solid and strong but tender as well.

Was there anything more attractive than a strong man who could also be gentle?

That's what she was thinking as she softly closed the door, not even allowing a click as she carefully twisted the knob before closing it and letting it go gently.

She turned, figuring to walk to the stairs, but she hadn't realized that Derek had stopped right beside her, and she ran into him, her head down, thumping him in the chest, and she again bit back a startled yelp.

"I'm sorry!" she exclaimed softly.

His hands came up, holding her on either arm, seeming to help her get her balance. "Are you okay?"

"I'm fine," she murmured. *Just embarrassed.*

"I'm guessing your leg hurts. Is that what the problem is?"

There was true caring in his voice, like he was concerned about her. Of course, a friend would be too. But...she wanted to be more.

She had to let go of that.

His hands were warm and rough on her bare arms; she couldn't quite lift her face to look him in the eye but stared at his chin.

"No. It hurts, but I guess I'm just...thinking."

"She's a sweet girl," he said, and she remembered that she had confided in him how badly she wanted children.

He assumed that she was thinking about having a child of her own. Which is probably what she would have been doing if he hadn't been here with her. She hadn't even given it too much thought, not with Derek taking up all of her brain. Admiring him, watching him, thinking about how good he was with children, what a great father he'd be.

That's what she wanted.

"Rose?" Derek said softly.

She lifted her brows, but he didn't say anything, and so she forced her head up a little, just enough to meet his eyes. "What?"

"You were amazing with her this evening. It's pretty incredible how she trusts you and is so comfortable with you. And you seem to anticipate her needs and meet them. It was a pleasure to watch."

She hadn't realized he was watching her. Funny, because she had been watching him.

"You were pretty good with her too. I... I think you will be a wonderful dad." Maybe she shouldn't have said that, and she bit her tongue before she said more.

He swallowed, his mouth opening just a little as though he were going to speak, but no words came out as they stood and stared at each other.

His hands loosened some around her arms, and his fingers lightly brushed over them, so soft and gentle she wasn't sure she was feeling it and not imagining it.

"Rose, I..." He didn't say anything more but moved closer, one hand going up around her neck as he lowered his head.

Her stomach dipped and twirled, and her hands reached up without her even thinking about it to settle on either side of his hard waist. Maybe, maybe he was feeling the same way she was.

Her eyes fluttered closed as his head lowered toward hers.

The sound of the front door opening broke them apart.

Her hands dropped from his waist, and he stepped back, his arms going to his sides.

She blinked a little, disoriented.

Disappointed.

The sound of her sisters chattering downstairs as they walked in drifted up to the hall.

"I better hurry down and tell them they need to be quiet."

"Yeah. That's a good idea. And I... I'd better go. It's late."

"Thank you for being willing to shift gears and not do what we were expecting," she said.

"I don't recall a date where I had more fun than this one. So, I guess being willing to shift gears has a lot of advantages."

She smiled. He truly had seemed to have had a good time. It made the glow in her chest burn warmer.

"I had a great time too. Best date ever." She smiled back at him, looking over her shoulder as her hand held onto the banister.

They stared at each other for just a moment before she started down the steps.

There wouldn't be any privacy once they stepped into the room with her sisters, and Derek was right. He needed to go. It was late, and he had animals to feed in the morning.

He greeted her sisters, who gave them curious glances as they came down the stairs until Rose explained that they had been putting Naomi to bed.

Derek chatted for a few minutes, and then he left, and although she wanted to ask him to text her when he got home so that she knew he got home safely, she didn't.

She hadn't been lying, though, when she said it was the best date of her life.

Chapter 15

So many things...base your marriage on faith in God. Stand by your vows. Love is a choice, not just a feeling. Choose love, even in the hard times and there will be hard times. Remember no one is perfect, even you. Learn to forgive quickly. (We have been married 60 yrs. next week)
- Judy Huffman from SE Ohio

Sunday morning, Rose still had little Naomi. That wasn't totally unusual, since there had been several times where Becky had just dropped Naomi off and didn't pick her up for several days.

Rose didn't mind.

She was allowing Naomi to fix her hair as they were getting ready for Sunday school when her phone buzzed with a text.

Can I pick you up for church?

She smiled. It was Derek.

He texted her several times, and they'd seen each other a little when she was out helping his grandma, but she'd had Naomi with her, and he'd been busy outside, and they hadn't talked to each other much.

She picked up her phone. **I have to be there early because I teach Sunday school.**

Just tell me what time to pick you up.

She sent him the time she normally left and looked at what Naomi was doing to her hair in the mirror.

"That looks pretty," she said. Unsure exactly what Naomi was doing, maybe imitating a braid, as she pulled strands of hair and wrapped them around each other.

"It won't stay in." Naomi's lip came out.

"Here. Let me show you."

She hadn't planned on going to church with braids in her hair, but she figured it wouldn't hurt if it made Naomi happy. Pulling all her hair around in the back and starting up by her neck, she braided it, waiting until the braid was long enough for it to come over her shoulder, and then she said, "You put one strand over top of the other, and you switch from hand to hand. It's kind of hard to do by yourself when you're little. But I can help you if you want."

Naomi smiled and nodded her chin up and down.

"Give me your hands," she said, opening up three fingers while she used her thumb and first finger to hold on to the braid.

Naomi put her little hands in hers, and they worked on braiding the rest of her hair together.

After Rose had tied it off, she smiled at Naomi. "Would you like me to fix your hair so that it matches mine?"

Naomi nodded eagerly, so Rose got up out of the seat and helped Naomi up, fixing her hair so that it hung in one braid down her back.

"There. Now we match."

"Now I look like you." Naomi looked proud and happy, and Rose's heart swelled.

She didn't care what her hair looked like, never had, but being able to love and help a little one made her feel like she was doing everything she had been born to do.

The old thoughts of it not being fair, why Becky would have a child when Rose had been denied, wanted to surface and bring her down, but she shoved them aside.

If she had her own children, she wouldn't be able to give Naomi this one-on-one attention.

"We better get moving, Mr. Derek will be here any minute to pick us up."

Rose held her hand out, and Naomi put her little hand in hers, and they walked out of the room together.

They'd eaten breakfast earlier, and several of her sisters were already back downstairs after getting dressed, but Derek pulled up right as they came down, so they put their coats on and were at the door in time to meet him.

"I thought I'd have to wait on you," he said, opening the door as they stepped out.

"You're right on time, so why would you have to wait?"

"It's just been my experience that when a woman says one time, what she actually means is a half an hour, at least, in the future."

"We'll try not to do that. I can't say I'm never late though." She grinned down at Naomi. "Right?"

The little girl nodded her chin up and down. "Right!"

"We can go in my car if you want. That's where the car seat is." They'd had to pick it up from Becky's house on their date earlier in the week.

"I'll move it to my truck, if that's okay with you."

"It is."

They moved everything and got Naomi buckled in and soon were headed down the highway toward the church.

They hadn't said anything for a while, as Naomi chattered in the background.

Rose had her hands clasped in her lap, tightly gripping her Sunday school bag with all the materials she needed in it, while she thought about what she would say. She didn't want another week to go by without correcting her lie, but she wasn't looking forward to having to face people, admitting what she'd done.

It wasn't necessarily that she was concerned about what Harry and Leah would think of her, but it was more the idea that she didn't want to humble herself in front of them.

Admitting that she was wrong, that she had sinned, put her at a disadvantage.

Although she knew that in God's equation, somehow when someone humbled themselves, God lifted them up.

She didn't really understand it, but she also knew that if a person sinned, they had to make it right.

"You're quiet," Derek said as Naomi took a couple of moments to breathe and the chatter stopped for a bit.

"I know. I'm sorry." She didn't want to not talk to him. She'd had such a good time on their date. And honestly, she'd been disappointed that he hadn't kissed her.

But maybe he'd been glad they were interrupted. He hadn't said anything. And she had no reason to think it had been something he wanted to repeat.

But maybe he did, the optimistic side of her brain insisted. It wanted to go through all the reasons why she was wrong when she thought he might be glad that he had ended up not kissing her. After all, he was here taking her to church.

But they'd agreed to date. So, although she didn't exactly expect him to, it didn't shock her that he was.

"Is it something I can help you with?"

"No. I'm planning on talking to Harry and Leah and apologizing for lying, and I suppose any time you plan on doing something like that, most of you doesn't want to."

"Amen to that." Derek's hands flexed on the steering wheel, and he didn't say anything else. He didn't need to. His tone had conveyed that he knew exactly how she felt. And there really wasn't anything he could do. "I can stand beside you while you do it."

She looked across the seat, not expecting that. Although she didn't know what she thought he would do—try to stay as far away from her as possible? Maybe. After all, she was going to be embarrassing herself, and people usually didn't seek out embarrassment or hang around people who were seeking it out.

Naomi started chatting again, and they didn't say much more as they pulled into the church.

After getting Naomi out, they each held one of her hands and she walked between them toward the basement door.

They greeted Ty and Louise and Palmer and Ames who were headed toward the same place.

Normally, Harry and Leah didn't make it for Sunday school, and this Sunday was no exception.

Rose taught her class, but she wished she had been able to get her confession over with so she didn't have it hanging over her head. It was hard to forget, and part of her thought that maybe she didn't do a very good job teaching since she couldn't get the writhing snakes to stay still in her belly.

Normally, Sunday school went fast and she could never believe that it was over.

But today, she must have looked at the clock one hundred times and couldn't believe how slow it was going.

Finally though, the teachers for junior church came to pick up the kids to take them to class, and she cleaned up her classroom. Looking around at the little desks all neatly cleared off, she turned off the lights and walked out.

Perfect timing since Harry and Leah were walking in the door.

Rose lifted her chin, wishing that somehow Derek would know to come downstairs from the men's class to stand beside her. She hadn't accepted his offer and now wished she'd been clear that she would welcome his support.

Suddenly she was scared, nervous, and thinking, *Does it really matter whether I apologize? We've already taken care of the lie.*

But she needed to. She'd lied. She needed to confess the lie, not cover it.

The door to the steps opened. She glanced over her shoulder and saw Derek walking through it.

Like he'd heard her call him mentally, he'd come down.

More likely the men's class was over, and he'd come down to help her clean up her room or maybe just to walk upstairs with her.

Whatever it was, she was relieved that he would be coming up behind her as she faced Harry and Leah.

"Harry, Leah, hello," she said, her voice trembling and breathy from the nervousness that had only gotten worse during Sunday school.

"Rose," Leah said, struggling with one of the children as she tried to yank his coat off but his arm appeared to be stuck.

Rose bent down, straightening his elbow so the sleeve didn't catch anymore, and the coat slipped off.

The kid didn't look at her but ran toward the junior church room, catching up with his siblings.

Rose straightened, a little smile on her face at the eagerness of the child to be in junior church and her hands only trembling a little.

She squeezed them together.

"I need to talk to you two," she said, her mouth suddenly dry and her eyes wanting to do nothing but blink.

"What?" Harry said, smirking a little. "If you need Leah to give you pointers on how to catch a man, I'm sure she'd be happy to."

Rose clamped her teeth down on her tongue and counted to five. She'd "caught" a man. The problem was she wanted to catch a man who knew how to keep his word. And Leah couldn't give her any pointers on that.

"Actually, I wanted to admit that I told you guys a lie."

That made both of them look at her sharply.

She felt a weight on her shoulder, a warm hand gripping her and pulling her, her side connecting with hard warmth.

Derek. He had his arm around her and had pulled her to his side.

She fit nicely under his shoulder, and she allowed herself a couple of seconds of enjoyment before she looked at her ex and his wife.

"I told you at the sweethearts' banquet that I was seeing someone and we were practically engaged. That wasn't true."

Harry's smirk grew bigger, but Leah's face scrunched up and she looked between Rose and Derek.

"You guys look awfully cozy for not being together," she finally said, her voice flat, and she actually sounded like she didn't believe Rose.

"That's because we are." Derek's voice was firm, and he bent his head and dropped a kiss on Rose's head.

Maybe she had fallen in love with him when he was putting Naomi to bed. When he was so good with her, when he picked her up and put her on his shoulders so she could see the sow better, when he made pancakes with her. When he picked them up for church.

If what Rose was feeling wasn't love, she wasn't sure what it could possibly be instead. Her sisters had always had her back completely, but this was different.

This was someone who didn't have to defend her. He didn't have to be with her. He didn't have to be standing here, his arm around her, his action saying that she was special and important, which meant even more because they were standing in front of the man who had rejected her and the woman who had broken up her marriage.

She'd never felt anything this good in her life before.

"Then I don't understand. What's the lie?" Leah said.

Harry didn't look like he cared. Whether Rose lied or whether she didn't, he'd gotten the upper hand. He wasn't alone, and she was.

"It's what I said. When I told you I was with someone and we were serious, it wasn't true."

"You're with someone, but it's not serious?" Leah said, her voice still flat.

"She's with me. And maybe she's not serious, but I am. She has a beautiful heart, and I'm not going to let her go. Not if I can help it," Derek said, and he sounded serious. Honest. Like he meant every single word.

Rose's heart beat hard over the words, and that warmth she'd felt the night they put Naomi to bed together came back, filling her chest.

She couldn't look at him though. Everything she felt would be on her face.

"Then I don't understand what you're doing. It's not like you lied and it's not true," Leah said, and Rose figured she might as well let it go.

She'd confessed, and Leah had no clue as to what she was saying. Just the idea of making something right, of sinning and confessing it, was so foreign to her that what Rose was doing baffled her.

Maybe Harry understood, but his smirk didn't leave.

"It won't be for long," Harry said, looking at Derek. "She's boring, never wants to do anything or go anywhere, and she's not very good at…anything," he said, looking around at the church, his gaze seeming to say that he might have said something different if they hadn't been standing inside the building.

Rose figured it didn't matter whether they were in the church or not, it was a nasty comment, wherever they were.

Some people had the idea that being a Christian meant going to church, pretending to be something you weren't, and then acting like the rest of the world the rest of the week.

That really wasn't the kind of Christianity that Rose practiced, not that she was any better than anyone else.

It just wasn't what she wanted to be, wasn't what she thought God wanted her to be.

"Come on. Church is starting," Derek said, tugging on her shoulder, and she gave in to the pressure, turning with him easily and walking toward the door.

Harry and Leah didn't seem to follow them, since they walked through the door, and it closed behind them. They started walking up the stairs, but Derek stopped, standing beside her, still with his arm around her, and said, "You did the right thing. I'm proud of you."

"Thank you for standing beside me. It would have been easy for you to not."

"No. It was hard for me to stay up in class until it was over, because I was afraid you would meet them without me. In fact, I left early. I didn't want you to have to do that by yourself."

"Thank you." In unison, they paused, one foot on the next step, one foot on the one they were on, and looked at each other.

She wasn't sure exactly what was passing between them, but she felt like he was saying that he would be there, anytime she needed him. Anytime she had something hard to go through, he wasn't going to let her down or leave her.

Whether or not they kept going in their relationship, that was a good kind of friend to have. And maybe, it was a good kind of friendship to build a relationship on. Being with someone who wasn't going to desert her when it was inconvenient to be around her.

She had no idea what he was thinking, but she knew she was blessed.

The door opened behind them, though neither one of them looked back. They just started up the steps again and went and sat down.

Chapter 16

Work past the bumps in the road and open communication.
Worked for 60 years until he stepped into eternity.
- MaryAnn Engel

"I think we can do it," Derek said as they drove back to Sweetwater from the butcher shop they'd visited that afternoon.

"It didn't look hard at all. And, the idea that you can learn a lot of that online is really encouraging."

Rose, with her red cheeks and glowing face, looked as excited as he felt. He supposed he shouldn't be saying "we" since there was no official "we" after their dating end date. But she seemed just as interested as he was and asked just as many questions of the butcher shop owner.

There was the red tape - USDA had to be involved, and some definite guidelines and regulations. But beyond the building and the extra, room-sized cooler that would need to be built, it would be the same as putting up any other kind of building.

"I thought it would be a lot harder," he said, still not believing how easy it seemed like it would be.

"Me too. I guess maybe because I've never done anything with butchering. It seemed like a complicated process and something that not just anyone could do."

"I'm the same. Sure we grew our own meat on the farm, but we took it to the butcher, dropped it off, and that was it."

"I guess it's like anything else, we'll just work at it until we figure it out."

She looked across the seat. Their eyes met and they smiled before he looked back at the road, feeling good, confident, maybe not like he could conquer the world, but that he could conquer his corner of it.

Rose had asked questions he hadn't thought of, but that were good and showed she'd been thinking. He loved that even though she didn't have anything in it, nothing aside from knowing him, she'd thrown herself into it just to help him. Sure, they'd agreed to be together until the Dating Game, but he hardly thought that was it.

She just wasn't that kind person. She did things because they were right.

He thought about her confessing her lie to her ex and his wife. How hard that must have been. How much he admired her for having the courage to do that. How much he wanted to stand beside her and support her.

How proud he was of her.

She wanted to do the right thing, and she didn't let whether or not it was easy determine whether or not she did it.

That was the kind of person he wanted to be with. Whether he was talking about a friend, or whether he was talking about his wife. He wanted someone who was going to do right each and every time. Who would encourage him to do the same.

"You know, call me crazy, but I kinda miss Naomi. I almost wish Becky hadn't picked her up." He couldn't quite believe he was saying it, because people weren't supposed to enjoy having children around, but maybe just watching how happy it made Rose, or maybe because Naomi was such a good child, he wasn't sure.

"She is special, isn't she?" Rose said, and maybe there was just a little sadness in her voice, but she sounded mostly happy.

"Having Naomi reminded me of elementary school, and...do you remember being paired up with me for the science project that we did?"

"In first grade?" she said, looking over the seat at him, light seeming to dawn in her eyes like she had kinda forgotten about it until he said something.

"Yeah. I hadn't thought of that in years," she said.

"Me either. But Naomi just kind of looks like you, and even though she's not in school yet, when you wore your hair in a long braid on Sunday and Naomi matched you, it reminded me of that, because that's how you wore your hair then, or at least whatever I remember of it."

"You're right. I remember my mom braiding it every morning, because it was so long, it would get caught in everything and get knotty if she didn't."

"Yeah, well, maybe I never apologized for spilling all that Jell-O on you, but I guess I am now."

She laughed. "I actually didn't mind, because they let me go home. I was always looking for reasons to get out of school."

"Really? I loved school. I couldn't wait to get there every day."

"I was always trying to talk my mom into letting me stay home. I knew better than to lie and say I was sick, but I would tell her that she needed me to help around the house, or at the auction barn, or go get groceries with her. I even offered to clean the house. Usually she told me no."

"That's funny, school was my favorite thing ever. I hated summer, not hated exactly, because you got to sleep in, but I loved going to school."

"Did you spill that Jell-O on me on purpose?" She narrowed her eyes and looked at him like the thought just occurred to her.

"Maybe," he said, gritting his teeth. "Will you be mad at me if I say yes?"

"Is it the truth?"

"Yes?"

"Why?"

"I wanted to talk to you, and you were just quiet never said anything, and I figured if I spilled the Jell-O on you, that would break the ice, I guess."

"Wow. I'm glad your moves have changed slightly since then."

"What can I say, when you're seven, things like dumping Jell-O on a girl seem like a good idea."

"Wow. I think some people might have considered you hopeless."

"My mom always did act like I was the one who caused her the most grief out of all five of us."

"I think I caused my mom the least amount of grief. I was always happy just sitting around playing with my dolls. Although, one time Glory took one of my dolls and wouldn't give her back, and I'm pretty sure I brought the house down with my screaming."

"I can't imagine, but I believe you if you say so."

"Oh I say so. I don't think I've ever thrown a fit like that in my life. In fact I know I haven't. In fact, I don't really recall fighting with any of my siblings, ever, except that one time. They all fought with each other, but I was just happy in a corner with my doll babies and being a mom to them. And whichever sibling wasn't getting along with the rest of them, usually came over and played with me."

"But you got protective when one got stolen?"

"Kidnapped. It was kidnapped." She could hear the insistence in her voice. The same thing she'd screamed at her mom through her tears and almost hyperventilating, because her doll baby wasn't properly dressed and Glory had taken her outside in the cold.

"I guess it's a crazy thing now to throw a fit about, but I was almost inconsolable. In fact, I don't even think my mom tried to calm me down. She just went outside, got Glory, made her come in and give me my doll and apologize."

"I'm not sure my mom wouldn't have disciplined me for throwing such a big fit."

"My mom might have, but, really, I never threw fits. Ever. I did everything my parents wanted me to. They never had any problems with me at all, except for that one time. And it wasn't even because she took my doll. It was because she wasn't taking care of her."

"I suppose there's a difference, although kidnapping is a crime."

"I know. Sometimes I remind Glory of that, when she starts to put on airs." She looked over, batted her eyes a little, making herself smile and relax. Funny, how that memory could still get her a little worked up.

"Do you still have your dolls?"

"Oh, my goodness, yes. Although, they're safely put away in a chest. But, someday..." Someday she was going to have her daughters play with them. Maybe her daughters would want brand-new dolls, but then she would have dolls to play with.

"Someday maybe your girls would play with them?" he asked softly like he'd read her mind.

She pulled her eyes away from the snow-covered North Dakota fields, looked over and nodded, her throat tight, her heart full.

He understood.

"You know, I know we weren't really friends in school, and I left, went to The Cities for a decade, but have you ever been around someone for just a little bit and you click so closely that you feel like you've known them forever?"

He stared out the windshield, watching the road as he spoke, and she looked at his profile. Strong nose, square chin jaw, a little bit of stubble, enough to make him look rugged, enough to keep his face warm in the North Dakota wind, his chest was deep, his hand strong on the wheel.

He was a good man and she had to agree with him. She felt comfortable with him in a way that she didn't feel with too many people. Aside from the awkwardness of whatever relationship they had, he had stood by her when not many people she knew would have.

"Did you notice today, when we were talking to Mr. Pyne about the butcher shop, you asked questions, ones I hadn't thought of. It amazed me how you were coming at it from one angle, I came at it from another, and we ended up with five times as much information as we might have had, if it had just been one of us alone."

"You're right," he nodded, the truck slowing as they came to a stop sign. "You would ask questions I had never even thought of, but we needed to know. And I hadn't considered we might need to until you said something. And... Well. You're right. You'd ask a question which would make me think of something else, and instead of getting twice as much information, we got even more."

"Yeah. I agree with you, not just about feeling like I've known you forever, but also, I just feel like...like we get each other but we're not the same. We..."

"Complement each other?"

"Yeah. That."

He glanced over, sitting at the stop sign, and their eyes met. Maybe he was digesting what they had just said, because she certainly was. It was more than just tingling feelings. It was a soul deep connection that she'd never felt with anyone else.

"I would never have said I believe in soulmates," she started, then she clamped her mouth shut and looked away. She didn't mean that. Not that they were soulmates, exactly, but that's how she felt. That kind of connection.

"Me either. But that's what it feels like to me. You?" he asked, insecurity hitting that last word hard.

"Yeah," she said softly.

He looked in the rearview mirror, like his eyes were pulled there. "I've created a traffic jam. There are two cars behind us."

"You'd better get going. This will make the papers if we get another one."

They laughed, and he turned, going toward the auction barn where they were going to help unload three different trailers of animals that had come in which her mom had texted them about.

"Maybe we can talk about that later?" he asked, his jaw flexing a little.

"Please. I'd like to."

Chapter 17

*Compromise. No one can win all the arguments. And prior-
itize what is important, no use in arguing over the color of
the couch!*
- Cathy Beecher from Coxsackie, NY

They got out at the auction barn, and Derek wished they hadn't
agreed to help.

Not that he didn't enjoy it, not that he minded, but he'd wanted
to pursue that conversation with Rose. He thought they were on
the same page, and their relationship had been so rocky from the
beginning, he wanted to get it straightened away.

Wanted to make sure that Rose understood he wanted her for
more than a month, wanted a lifetime, maybe.

Maybe?

No. There were no maybes. He had never felt this sure about
anything.

But it might scare her if she realized how strongly he felt about
it. About her.

It was going to have to wait, anyway, since they were here and
had cows to move.

He opened the door. She walked in first, giving him a little smile
as she passed him and saying thank you.

It was a courtesy she hadn't had to show, although maybe he
hadn't had to hold the door open for her, either.

Maybe that was part of being friends, mutual respect, and not
just one friend always giving while another was always taking.

Not that those kinds of relationships were bad, because biblically, God never said to ditch people who didn't give him stuff. But, he figured the very best friendships were ones where both people were working to make it better.

He felt that's what Rose did.

"Hey, guys," one of Rose's sisters shouted. He thought it might be Glory. "We've gotten this mama cow and her baby out of the trailer. We want to put them in the last pen in the middle row." Glory moved quickly to shut gates to direct the cow where she wanted.

"Watch out. That mom is pretty protective of her little one," her mom called from the side of the trailer where the cow and calf were getting off.

"Hey, Rose, how did things go today?" Coleman asked from the catwalk above them.

Rose stopped and looked up, but Derek kept moving. He could see the gate Glory was working on had gotten jammed somehow, and she wasn't going to get it closed in time. Maybe there had been a chain around it that she hadn't seen.

The calf went flying by, and Glory quit working on the gate, instead jumping up as the mama went by close enough that if Glory hadn't moved, the mama would have hit her.

Derek had been around enough mama cows to know that his best bet was to just get out of the way. She was scared, in an unknown place, and her baby was running ahead of her, so she'd be running after him. There was no point trying to stop her. So he jumped up on the fence as she went by as well.

She hadn't gotten as close to him. But then, instead of going straight, the calf veered off and went down the aisle that Derek had just come from, where Rose was standing with her back to it, looking up at her brother, who had scrunched down on his haunches, and looked straight down at her as they spoke.

The calf stopped for a minute, and Derek thought maybe she was turning around, but as the mama came around the corner and started up toward it, the sound startled the calf again, and it took off.

"Watch out!" he said immediately, as the cow tore off after the calf, straight up past Glory.

The calf ran by her with no issues, but Rose hadn't moved, hadn't even turned around to look, and the cow was heading straight toward her.

"Rose! Move!" Derek yelled, running toward her, knowing he was going to be too late; he was following the cow after all.

The cow had her head down and was just a few feet from Rose when she turned at his shout.

Her eyes got big, and she glanced around, almost like she was trying to decide which way to go, before she ran to the closest side, her arms slapping the top board of the fence trying to get up.

She didn't make it, and the cow ran straight into her, slamming her against the fence with its head, but barely slowing down as it kept running.

Coleman dropped down from the catwalk less than a second after the cow went by. He reached Rose's side at the same time Derek did.

"Are you okay?"

"I'm fine. Everything works." She huffed out a breath, laughing a little, and blinking.

"You got her?" Coleman said softly, although his voice was hard.

"Yeah," Derek replied.

Coleman didn't say anything else, but jogged away, moving up the aisle, making sure the cow wouldn't come back while Derek took care of Rose.

"Seriously. She just plowed into you. Surely it hurts somewhere?" He took a hold of her shoulders, trying to get her to look in his eyes. Looking over her front, like there would be some kind of blood or something.

"No. Really. The worst thing that hurts is my cheek."

He hadn't even looked at her face. But the cow ramming into her must have jerked her head against the board because there was a brush burn right below her eye.

He reached his hand up, and she flinched a little. He touched her cheek gently just below her eye.

"Not bleeding, but it looks like it hurts. Burns."

"That's what it feels like," she said softly. "Thanks a lot for yelling at me. I never heard it."

"You guys looked like you were in a pretty deep discussion."

"He wanted to know about the butcher shop, and this dude that he knows with the buffalo wants an answer." She smiled a little sheepishly. "Coleman really wanted to talk to you." She lifted her brows and tilted her head. "But I'm glad you didn't stop. Or that would have been you against the fence."

"I would rather it had been." His words came out a little fiercely. "Think my heart jumped out of my chest, and I'm not sure I would have been able to get it back in if something would have happened to you."

That was a cheesy line. It sounded dumb. But it was true. He'd been scared to death that something was going to happen to her.

He lifted his hand up. "My fingers are still shaking."

Her eyes moved to his fingers, confirming that they were indeed shaking, before she said, "I'm okay. Truly."

"I know. You look fine. You're sure nothing hurts?"

"No. Nothing that important anyway."

"Don't scare me like that again," he said, knowing she couldn't make any promises to that effect, but he slid his hand around her neck and stepped closer.

Her hands came up, wrapping around his shoulders, and he took that to mean she was okay with what they were doing.

Because he had every intention of kissing her this time and not being interrupted. Not by anything.

Except maybe a charging cow.

He almost looked both ways, just to make sure that nothing was coming, but instead he said, "The other night when we put Naomi to bed, I wanted to kiss you. And I was frustrated with myself the rest of the night because I left without doing it."

"I was disappointed too."

Her words made him smile a little, and his thumb moved over the short hairs of her neck.

Those words also gave him the courage he needed to lower his head. His lips touched hers, her arms tightened around his shoulders, and he pulled her close to him, deepening the kiss and forgetting they were in the auction barn, that there was an angry mama cow running around somewhere, that her family could see them, that he hadn't even known her that long, that their relationship wasn't even supposed to be real...none of it mattered.

It was the best kiss he'd ever had.

And as he raised his head, noting that her breathing was just as trembly as his, he said, "I don't want to have an end date on our relationship. I want it, forever."

She smiled, not saying anything, raising her head again, moving it up and touching her lips to his.

He took that as a sign that maybe she didn't want to talk just then.

Chapter 18

Address a problem immediately and never use sarcasm in
your response. Sarcasm is disguised anger, and is designed to
attack and denigrate the other person's opinions or outlook.
- Carolyn Veith from New Hampshire

T he fire hall was crowded; all the seats were filled and it seemed like there were people everywhere. The air felt alive with excitement. This was the first time they'd done this type of format for the Dating Game, and the Piece Makers were all there in force. There must have been twenty ladies wearing their purple and orange sweatshirts.

Charlene wasn't hard to pick out with her blue hair waving gently as she adjusted microphones and made sure all the contestants were ready.

Rose couldn't believe her hands were sweating and her heart seemed to be skipping every other beat on a pretty regular basis.

Why was she nervous?

She had answered all the questions that they'd given her and they'd written them down on cards. Now she was back out sitting at one of the four tables in the front waiting on Derek to finish answering his questions and come out and join her.

Maybe she'd be less nervous if he were beside her.

That was a sure thing since over the past few weeks they'd gotten very comfortable with each other. So comfortable that he felt like a natural part of her.

They'd had Naomi a few times too, and it never bothered him to cancel whatever they were doing so they could do whatever they needed to with her. Or they'd just take her with them.

"All right everyone, here come the men!" Charlene said into the microphone, her voice excited and stirring up the crowd even more.

Vicki showed the men where to sit, organizing things like she'd raised six boys. Which she had.

The chaos didn't seem to bother her. She was as cool and unruffled as anyone could be.

Kathy set down a bunch of cards in front of Rose and said, "Don't touch these. They have all your answers on them and they should be in the correct order. All you need to do whenever you're prompted is to hold up the top card. Make sure you don't grab two."

Rose nodded, gratified when Derek finally came and sat down. He nodded at her and smiled, but didn't say anything, because they'd been instructed not to speak to each other.

Things were starting right away, so they wouldn't have time to put their heads together and compare answers.

Aside from Harry and Leah, Brawley, one of the Powers brothers, the most outgoing one, had been paired with the shy billing clerk from the hospital, Cassie.

Rose didn't think she'd ever heard Cassie say more than three sentences in a day before, and Brawley would be her total opposite.

They were the couple that weren't actually a couple. They didn't even really know each other, other than seeing each other around town.

She and Derek were the couple that had been together for a short time.

Then Harry and Leah were the couple that had been married for a short time, and Sawyer and Georgia were the couple that had been married for ten years.

The Piece Makers had thought it might be fun to see if a couple who wasn't even a couple might be able to beat a couple who have been married for a long time.

It just seemed like a neat idea to have different couples from different stages in their relationships – two who were married, two who weren't - and see if being together for a long time truly made a difference.

Sawyer looked completely confident, and his Georgia, tiny with wild curly hair, looked happy and glowing. He smiled at her benevolently and she had visibly relaxed when he came out with her questions answered.

If Rose ever doubted whether people could stay in love for a long time, all she had to do was look at Sawyer and Georgia. They could make anyone believe in the power of love.

Charlene stood at the front, and began. "I wanted to welcome everyone here today. Thank you all for coming. Thank you for supporting us. All proceeds from this will be used to buy materials so we can make quilts and other supplies for people who are in need - in our town, and anywhere else."

She went on to introduce all the couples, mention how long they'd been together. The crowd tittered as she introduced Brawley and Cassie, who had never been together at all, and from the look on Cassie's face, she wished she were anywhere else.

Rose had no idea how anyone might have talked her into it, although if anyone could talk anyone into anything, Charlene would be the one.

Charlene finished with her announcements, and she handed the microphone over to Vicki.

Vicki took it and said, "All right. Let's get started."

"For question number one we asked all contestants what their favorite color is. A very civil question, right?"" The crowd laughed, and so did Vicki. "Let's see how they did," Vicki's voice made it sound like she knew that some of them didn't get the answers right.

Colors weren't something that Derek and she had talked about, and Rose actually wasn't sure whether she got the right answer. She'd picked something that made sense to her, as she looked back thinking about the clothes he wore, but she didn't know for sure.

They started out with Brawley and Cassie. Cassie must have done what Rose did and picked the color that made sense. Her answer was "blue."

It matched what Brawley had just held up on his card, and Rose wasn't quite sure whether that was a smile on Cassie's face or not, because she still looked nervous and like she'd rather be anywhere else. Brawley on the other hand, must have picked his favorite color for Cassie, because he held a card that said "blue" as well.

Cassie said green.

Harry and Leah got both colors right, which didn't surprise Rose at all. Favorite colors usually came up in a marriage at some point, whether it was decorating, or buying furniture, or even a blanket for the couch.

Sawyer and Georgia got theirs right as well.

"All right Rose and Derek, you're the fourth couple. Let's see how you did. Derek what's your favorite color?"

Derek grinned with confidence and said, "Brown."

Rose smiled and held up her card. "Brown."

The crowd clapped, and Rose smiled big.

Derek's eyes widened, like he was surprised she'd picked up on it, and she shrugged, unable to talk to him, but wanting to tell him that every shirt he owned was brown, so she just took an educated guess.

"That was good," Vicki said. "Rose, he looked surprised you knew."

"That's because I am." Derek said honestly. The crowd laughed.

"What is your favorite color Rose? Let's see if Derek can guess as well as you."

"Purple," Rose said, still smiling, but not expecting him to have guessed. The only clue he might have had was her purple comforter, which she wasn't sure he'd seen the night they put Naomi to bed and the things that she had bought for Naomi. Naomi hadn't expressed a preference in colors, and so Rose bought purple whenever she could.

"Purple," Derek said.

Rose laughed, because he had picked up on it. It made her feel like he really paid attention to her.

She supposed if he hadn't gotten it right, she'd feel the exact opposite. That's why this game could be so dangerous. She didn't want to set a whole bunch of store in whether or not he knew the answers to questions that probably didn't matter much since they hadn't come up in their relationship.

There had been ten questions they'd answered, and they went rather quickly through them. Still it took more than an hour to get through seven, and at that point, Sawyer and Georgia were well ahead of everyone.

"All right, the next question is "What does her mother make that you hate?" This was a question only the men answered, obviously," Vicki said with a grin.

Brawley guessed something weird, since he had never eaten Cassie's mother's food, not just because they weren't a couple, but because her mother had passed away years ago.

Cassie answered honestly and by saying, "There is nothing she makes that he doesn't like."

Harry and Leah ended up in an argument because Harry mentioned five different dishes that her mother made that he couldn't stand. It wasn't the first argument they'd been in during the game, since Leah had been offended when he had no idea what her favorite flower was. She also got upset when he hadn't known her ideal honeymoon destination.

It wasn't where they had gone for their actual honeymoon.

Still, they didn't get a point, because Leah's answer had been that Harry loved everything her mother made.

Rose figured there would be some interesting conversations in their home this evening, which didn't exactly make her happy. Even though they'd broken up her marriage in order for them to be together, she didn't wish ill on them.

"All right Derek, it's your turn." Vicki looked at the two of them.

"Her mother doesn't make anything I don't like," Derek said.

Rose hid a smile. They'd gone first sometimes, and last sometimes and this just happened to be a time they were going last, so maybe he had learned from Brawley's experience that it was probably just best to say something that was true rather than make a wild guess.

Their answers matched rather closely, because *so far* he had liked everything her mother had made.

Her mother had only cooked one meal for them, since usually
Rose was the one who did the cooking, especially when Derek was
over.

They got a point for their matching answers.

They shared a ironic look, since both of them knew that they
were talking about one meal.

"All right. One more question. It looks like Sawyer and Georgia
are going to win handily - and there you go folks, after you've been
married for a while, you have a tendency to know your mate a lot
better." There was applause before she continued. "But, Rose and
Derek are in a strong second place. Although if neither one of them
get this answer, and Harry and Leah both get it... Well. Leah and
Harry still won't win."

The crowd laughed.

"But they'll not lose by as much," Vicki said, like that meant
something. "And, I'm not sure about Brawley and Cassie, but I
don't think you two have a future together." Vicki didn't say it
unkindly, and the crowd laughed again.

Cassie's face was red, and Brawley grinned good-naturedly. He
seemed completely unaffected, but Cassie's desire to leave the
building and go somewhere where she could crawl under a rock
seemed to be getting stronger.

Rose felt bad for her. From the little bit that they'd talked, Cassie
seemed to be a really nice person who would do anything for
anyone, but she was a strong introvert, and probably shy too.

Perfect for this game, and perfectly matched with Brawley, but
just watching her was uncomfortable to the point of pain.

"And now for the last question: Derek, what did Rose say is one
question you would like to ask her but never have?" Vicki said,
sounding a little triumphant, like this was a question that was sure
to stump everyone.

Derek's eyes glittered, although his mouth tilted. Almost as
though he was excited about his answer, but didn't have any idea
of what hers might have been.

She hadn't been sure of what to say. If she had a question to ask
him, she didn't beat around the bush about it. She didn't want to
be in a relationship where she was afraid to ask questions.

Kathy had been in charge of the timer, and they had the backup shot clock from the high school, so it was up behind their heads. The crowd could see the seconds ticking down as Derek hesitated.

Finally, when there was just one second left, he blurted out, "How old are you?"

After a chuckle, like that shouldn't be something they didn't know, Vicki pointed to Rose. "Show us your answer, Rose. Last card."

Rose held up her card. "When is your birthday?"

It was kind of the same, because since they graduated together and she knew how old he was, kinda. But that she didn't know when his birthday was, and she wasn't entirely sure exactly how old he was.

She grinned sheepishly. "I was never afraid to ask. I just never thought to."

"April 8th," he said immediately. Then he looked at Vicki. "We're allowed to talk now right?"

"Not yet." Vicki pointed to his card. "She has to guess your answer."

The shot clock started, and Rose's mind went blank. She couldn't think of a single question he would be afraid to ask. Then she figured she might as well be snarky if she couldn't be serious. So she said. "How many children do you want?"

Vicki laughed along with the crowd. She rolled her eyes a little. "That's a good one." She turned to Derek. "Hold your card up."

Derek's fingers fiddled with the edge of the card. Almost as though he'd answered the question but now he didn't want to show it to the entire room.

He slid his eyes over toward hers, and she thought with surprise that he truly was nervous. Her eyes widened, and she searched his face, trying to figure out what the world he might have said that he now wished he wouldn't have.

She tried to soften her gaze and let him know that whatever he said would be fine with her. She wasn't going to get upset about a question in a dating game.

Finally, he took a deep breath, swallowed with effort, and lifted the card.

The crowd gasped, while Rose craned her head to try to see since Vicki didn't read the question right away.

Finally, Vicki said, "I think this is one you'd better show her."

The other contestants couldn't see, and they all looked over, as Derek turned toward her with the card held in front of him.

Rose gasped, just as the crowd had, when she saw the card, and then something shiny caught her eye, and she looked at his pinky finger gripping the front of the card. A ring had been slid onto it down to the first knuckle where a diamond glittered on a golden band.

She read the sign again.

Would you marry me?

Her lungs weren't working, and she couldn't get a breath in, and her heart was doing some kind of calisthenics in her chest, but she managed to get out, "Yes!"

Another shaky breath. And louder she said, "Yes!" She smiled and stood. "I will!"

She took one step, and he met her, coming out of his chair, dropping the card as she threw her arms around him, and he gathered her close, bending his head and whispering, "I couldn't resist. I've been wanting to for a while. Even though it hasn't been long, I feel like I've known you forever, and I can't imagine ever letting you go."

"She already said yes. Kiss her," Vicki said, and the crowd erupted, as he lowered his head and touched his lips with hers.

Chapter 19

Living in God's word.
- Joanne Edwards from Jemison, AL

They decided to have a small wedding on Derek's birthday.
April 8th.

Why not?

Neither one of them wanted to wait.

But they did want to invite the whole town, so while they had a small ceremony, they made sure the entire town could come to the reception which they had at the fire station community building.

Brawley seemed like the perfect person to emcee the event, and he did a great job.

Rose couldn't look at Cassie without thinking about her paired up with Brawley at the dating game and feeling a little stirring of sympathy. Cassie was a great sport, and super nice, and had played along, hamming it up for the crowd maybe a little, but still, she figured that it would probably take a bulldozer and two world armies to get her to do a dating game again.

But it was Glory that really had her worried. She'd just seemed a little sad and depressed and Rose was concerned that Glory might decide to leave the family business. She'd made a few comments. Things that made Rose feel like she was being left behind with her older sisters getting married and that maybe she needed to go somewhere where she could feel more fulfilled.

Rose didn't want the family to be split up, but she didn't know anyone who Glory would be interested in. Not that she needed a man to keep her here, but it seemed like something that would work. A beautiful romance could make the world look like a better place.

"You look kind of angry? Are you having second thoughts?" Derek's voice cut into her thoughts.

She let out a breath, laughing a little and looking apologetic at him. "I'm sorry. I'm not angry at all, just thinking, and I know I kind of have a very serious thinking face."

"Are you sure?" Derek said, tilting his head and looking at her like he thought she might be holding out on him.

"I am." She smiled at him to show she truly had just been so far in her head she'd forgotten where she was.

"Okay," he said easily. "I hope it's okay with you, but I wanted to dance with my wife. Maybe you have some time?"

"I always have time for you," she said, looking up at him.

"Good to hear. Although, with those children that we're going to be having, I don't know if you will always be able to keep that promise."

"You come first," she assured him. Knowing that that was the way it had to be.

Their children would need her, of course they would. But she always needed to put her husband and her relationship with him before anything else. Even the kids. It was a good example for them, and also it was where her priorities needed to be.

The music began, and Derek took her hand, leading her to the dance floor. But before they made it, they were stopped by his Gram and Pap, who stood with someone Rose vaguely recognized as the hired guy who had worked for them before Derek came back from The Cities.

Rose's stomach cramped. She didn't want any trouble at their wedding.

Derek and she had decided to go in with the buffalo and had gotten things rolling with setting up the butcher shop, and she wanted to be able to move ahead with that. Not be reminded of all the mistakes they'd made, since he'd explained to her what happened with the hired guy and the stolen funds, but had asked her to keep it to herself, since his grandparents didn't want to embarrass or upset the family, especially considering his Gram was such good friends with the man's mother.

"Can I talk to you two for a moment? I know it's your wedding day," his Gram said, stopping in front of them. His Pap stood a little behind the hired guy, with his hand on his right shoulder, lending support.

"Of course," Derek said, glancing at Rose who nodded.

"I'm not sure you've ever met Bud?" she asked Rose, looking at her.

"I've seen him around town. I know who he is, but I'd forgotten his name."

Bud held out his hand. "Good to meet you Rose. You've got a good man."

She shook his hand, looking him in the eye and saying, "Thank you."

"I don't know if Derek explained to you what happened with Bud and his mother and our farm?"

Rose nodded. "He told me about it."

"I told her, but neither one of us said a word to anyone else," Derek said, his voice low, glancing around to make sure there was no one close.

"Well, I had something to say to you and to your grandparents, and I wanted to say it to you as well, since it affects you both."

Bud shifted, running a hand through his hair then shoving it into his pocket, obviously nervous. Then he cleared his throat and said, "I stole money from your grandparents. It was to pay for my mom's cancer treatments. What I didn't know, what I just found out a couple of days ago, is that mom had an insurance policy. It was a pretty big one. The first thing I want to do with the money that I'm getting from it is to pay your grandparents back. Every single cent that I took from them, with interest if they wanted."

"We already told you we don't want interest," Pap said firmly.

"Wow," Rose said softly.

"That's pretty amazing," Derek said, and there was true amazement in his voice.

Which, when he'd told her what his gram and pap did, he'd said how awed he was and how they'd handled it like a Christian should, rather than doing what everyone else in the world might have told them to do. Doing the hard thing and handling it with grace and beauty and love. Modeling what Jesus said - to love your enemies, and to forgive those who trespass against you. His grandparents had shown that as an example.

They talked for a bit more, and then his grandparents shooed them away, saying they didn't want to take any more of their time on their wedding day, but they'd talk more about what they needed to do on the farm in a few days.

Derek moved to put his arms around her. Maybe they swayed slowly to the music but he seemed preoccupied.

He lowered his head and said in her ear, "I couldn't believe what my grandparents had done. And now I can't believe how God has worked it out. Feels like a miracle, although I think sometimes the Lord just blesses those who follow him. Blesses people who do the hard things."

"I agree. Although, I don't think we always see the rewards here on earth."

"You're right. I think a lot of times the rewards are in heaven, and I can't help but think that, while I wouldn't call the six figures that Bud stole a piddling amount of money, I think the way God pays us back in heaven is a million times better and makes any amount of money here on earth look small in comparison."

"I agree. I agree so much, but...it's so hard to have that faith, that belief that God will actually do what He says. That He's actually as good as what He says. That He's actually faithful and just and will reward us, and that God's rewards are awesome."

"It seems too good to be true, so we don't think it is," Derek whispered beside her ear, shaking his head a little and grunting.

"You know, I guess that's how I feel about you. After my last marriage, I didn't think there was a man in the world who would love me, who would stay. Who would...treat me well. And I decided I just didn't want anyone. But you came along and you're better than I ever expected. More than I dreamed of. God...God really did reward me for taking the high road."

"Don't forget, He did the same to me. It's kind of funny how you feel like you're the one that's doing right, and they're the ones that are getting rewarded, but sometimes God just takes a little bit of time, maybe testing your faith to see if you believe before He gives you that amazing thing for doing what's right."

"I sure got it," she said looking up at him.

"I did too," he said, and they kissed on it.

Enjoy this preview of *Cowboy Coming Home,* just for you!

Cowboy Coming Home

Chapter 1

Do not be unequally yoked. Light can't mix with dark. Be God centered. God always first. Communication, commitment, loyalty, listening to each other's viewpoints and settling disagreements before going to bed.
- Ruth Carter from Warrenton, VA

Glory Baldwin didn't see the calf.

That was the problem.

Although, to be fair, the calf wasn't there when she put the cow in earlier.

Regardless, she should have been paying attention, but her sister Lavender had shouted, "Three more trailers just pulled in. We need that cow moved right away, and you need to come out and help us."

Glory had waved her hand, letting her sister know she'd heard, then she'd gone about moving the cow.

People were milling around in the penning area, but they were mostly people Glory knew, and they knew to stay out of the way when they were moving animals. The livestock auction that her family ran was scheduled to start ten minutes ago, but typically they didn't start on time. Usually people were still arriving with their animals at the start time.

Which is what was happening now, and Glory needed to move this single cow into a pen with several others so they had this pen for a herd of goats that was on a trailer right now waiting to be unloaded.

The new guy had put the cow in, and he put it in the goat area. Which had been fine before the goats had arrived and needed it.

Glory wasn't watching when she opened the gate and walked in the pen. It was way too big for a single cow anyway. They used it for goat herds.

Making a note that the light bulb above the pen was out, and it would need to be replaced tomorrow, she walked in, glancing out of the pen and down the aisle at her sister who was heading toward the unloading area.

Maybe the dim lighting was the reason she didn't see the calf lying in the straw.

Wet, but with the afterbirth cleaned off.

"Look out!" a deep male voice said, drawing her attention away from the calf that had just caught her eye—her brain hadn't had time to process what it was and where it came from—and toward the voice rather than toward the cow.

Out of her peripheral vision, she saw the cow coming for her.

Sometimes things happened and it felt like they were happening in slow motion in a person's head, while real life never slowed down.

That was one of those times for Glory. Since she knew the cow was coming, and she knew her feet needed to run, but she hadn't gotten the signal from her brain to her feet, and she stood rooted to the floor for what felt like five minutes but was probably only a second or so.

A body came from her left, plowing into the neck of the cow, just as the black head came within inches of Glory's stomach.

Her feet finally got the memo, and she ran to the side of the pen, one foot on the bottom board, but she didn't throw herself over; instead, she glanced over her shoulder to see what became of the person who had attacked the cow that was attacking her.

Later maybe she would shake her head over that one. Working in a sale barn, she would have said she'd seen everything.

This wasn't the first time she'd been attacked by a cow, but it probably was one of the closer times, and all because she hadn't been paying attention.

Growing up, her dad always, always told her, "Keep your eye on the cow. Don't ever take your eye off the cow."

She hadn't listened.

It hadn't gotten her, but some other one might.

The man, tall, wearing a T-shirt and faded jeans, with square-toed cowboy boots, and a ball cap, had run into the cow, knocking her off course enough for Glory to get away.

But the way the cow had turned when he hit her had knocked the man off balance, and Glory turned in time to see him sprawled on the ground, rolling immediately toward the fence.

Smart man, not taking the time to get up. Except, this was the goat pen, the fence was farther away than it usually was, and there wasn't enough room between the boards for the man to get through.

The cow, truly upset and scared now, and driven by instinct to do anything to protect her baby, stopped, glanced at the calf on the ground, then back to the man.

She lowered her head and ran toward him.

Glory saw it, but the cow had smashed the man into the fence as he'd started to stand to get over it and ground her head into his rib cage before Glory got a shout out of her mouth and was able to move herself forward.

She thought she heard a crack, but she hoped she was wrong. Because it was almost certainly the man's ribs.

Knowing that it should have been her getting smashed into the fence, if the man hadn't saved her, she couldn't turn away, even though the mama cow was scared and would almost certainly attack her as well.

At least she was on her feet and had a decent chance of getting away now that she was paying attention.

Hopefully, she could at least get the cow turned around. Surely, the shouting would get someone coming toward them. Someone to help, and if the man couldn't get himself up, someone would be there to drag him away if she could keep the cow away from him.

Her movement caused the cow to look at her but not leave the man. Glory knew what would draw the cow to her. She switched directions, and rather than lunging at the cow, she took three steps toward the calf.

The mama wanted to protect her baby, and nothing would draw a mama like something going toward her precious little one.

That was the instinct driving her now. And that was the instinct Glory played on.

She was no match for a sixteen-hundred-pound cow. But she liked to think her brain was bigger.

She was using it now, because brute strength wasn't going to get her anywhere.

Sure enough, the mama swung around, faster than one would think a clumsy cow would be able to swing, and charged toward the human by her baby.

Glory got out of the way, backpedaling as fast as she could. She smacked into the fence, her hands automatically gripping it and her foot going to the bottom rung.

The cow didn't chase her, standing over her calf, and she stood where she was, trying to see if the man could move.

The cow was in her way.

"Come on, mama," she said. "Come get me." She wasn't taunting. Well, maybe she was. She felt pretty secure in her position—secure that she could get over the fence before the mama got to her. But she didn't really want the mama to do that, because she'd want to turn back toward her calf right away, and the man might catch her eye.

Moving a little along the fence so she could see around the side of the cow, Glory caught movement in the dim back corner. At least the man wasn't dead.

She hadn't really thought he was, since the cow had gone after his chest.

That wouldn't kill him right away.

It would be more of a slow death.

He'd end up in the hospital with pneumonia, a punctured lung, internal injuries, and he'd never get better but just fade away.

Even strong, young, and healthy men sometimes couldn't pull through when their chest was smashed.

She'd seen it.

Thankfully, this cow didn't have horns, or the man might need an undertaker rather than an ambulance.

The cow hadn't moved, and Glory could see the man was up, one arm crossed high over his stomach, like he was keeping the pain in, and standing slightly hunched over, like straightening hurt, and he just couldn't do it. But rather than going to the gate or throwing himself over the fence, he was looking for her.

"Get on the other side," he said, his words strong but laced with pain.

Like a sturdy metal gate that was slightly rusted.

"I can make it before she gets to me," Glory said right away, not wanting the cow to turn around. She stood over top of her calf, and she'd probably be fine as long as no one made a move toward her. "You get out of there."

"You first," the man said, his tone commanding and brooking no argument.

She probably knew him, although she hadn't gotten a good look at him and still couldn't see, but most likely he was a rancher from the area. One she'd dealt with before. One whom she might even have gone to school with, although he definitely wasn't someone she worked with every week.

She'd recognize all of those; they were as familiar to her as her own brother.

Shoving her heel on the first fence board, she pushed up, keeping her face toward the cow, not giving her back.

That was the worst thing a person could do when they were chasing cattle and were worried a cow was going to charge—to give a cow their back. Cows might charge a person facing them, but they definitely would charge a person's back.

Apparently they'd never watched westerns.

As soon as her butt was on the top rung, she called out, "I'm good. You get out."

She wanted to be there if the cow moved or turned, because the man was in no condition to get away.

He glanced up, his face dark under his hat, but she could see the stubble and the dark eyes. He made sure she was out of danger before he climbed the fence, much slower than she had, swinging a leg over. Even from her position on the other side of the pen, she could see the pain he was in as he moved his body.

As soon as he had one leg over the fence, she figured at the very worst he could roll off the top, over to the other side, so she swung her legs around and hopped down, moving through the pen she had just landed in, past a herd of goats, who moved out of her way, hopping over that fence before she came around to look at the man.

The whole time, she was pulling her phone out of her pocket and calling Clint, who didn't miss an auction and was also a volunteer first responder. If a person in Sweet Water called the ambulance, he'd be the one going to get it. It seemed silly to call 911 to have an ambulance dispatched when Clint was here and could take this fellow to the hospital in his truck with the flashing blue light.

"Yeah," Clint answered his phone.

"Come down to the goat pens, please. I've got someone who's been smashed by a charging cow, and I think he probably has some broken ribs and possibly other injuries."

"On my way," Clint said, and she didn't bother to say goodbye, knowing he wouldn't.

"If that was for me, you're wasting your time," the man muttered as he came to the fence of the pen he was in, the two nannies who stood there with him eyeing him balefully.

"You're hurt. You need to get checked out."

"I'm fine," he said.

She wanted to roll her eyes. That was typical of men around here. They were "fine." They might have a severed artery and a knife sticking out of their heart, but they were fine. Always fine.

Like it was a badge of honor to not go to the hospital.

"Well, you're gonna have to get through my mom, because she's not going to want to find out that you got attacked by a cow and didn't go to the emergency room."

"Send her to me. I'll let her know," the man said, raising his eyes and looking for the first time full in Glory's face.

Armstrong Brandt.

She knew him, although he wasn't a regular at the sale. His wife had left him last summer, going back east, because she didn't feel fulfilled being a wife and mom and being stuck at home.

Maybe there was more to the story, but that's all Glory had heard. Immediately she started looking around for his little boys. Four of them. The oldest being six or eight. She wasn't sure.

And there they were. She'd been on her phone, and she hadn't seen them smashed back against the pen on the other side, their backs flush against it, their eyes wide.

Their dad had probably told them to get back and stay there, and the boys had listened.

"If you're worried about your boys, we can keep an eye on them. Someone will take care of them." She stopped short of saying she would do it herself. He might not appreciate that since she was the reason he was hurt to begin with. Also, of all the people in their family, Rose was the one who was great with kids. Not Glory.

They seemed to love Rose naturally, even if they'd never met her before.

Glory, not so much. She wasn't terrible with them, but it wasn't an automatic love as soon as they set eyes on her, the way it always was with Rose.

The man scrunched his face up. He'd gone through the gate of the pen and now stood in the aisle.

It wasn't hard to see from the set of his shoulders and the tension on his face that he was in a lot of pain.

"I take it Armstrong is the one who got attacked?" Clint said as he walked up to them.

"That's right. She got him pretty good. He was twisted, and she shoved him into the fence," Glory said, describing it as best she could, even though she'd seen it over her shoulder.

"I'll be fine. My ribs are a little bruised, but they'll be fine."

"I thought I heard a crack," Glory said.

Armstrong's eyes flew to hers. Like he had known about the crack but hadn't thought anyone else had heard.

"Then we definitely want to check that out, especially if there's a possibility they might be broken. You don't want to pierce a lung or get an infection. You can end up with more problems than just broken ribs," Clint said seriously, although he stayed with his hands in his pockets, a casual stance, because he knew as well as Glory did how stubborn men around the area could be. And that he was just as likely to not have a patient to take to the hospital as he was to have one. Unless they were unconscious, it wasn't a given.

"I'll be fine," the man insisted, a stubborn tilt to his chin, his eyes hard.

She'd heard Armstrong's ranch was successful, and she'd never heard of any problems associated with him, other than his wife walking out.

"What's going on?" Mrs. Baldwin, Glory's mom, stepped up.

"Nothing."

"He got smashed into the fence."

"I think Armstrong needs to go to the ER."

Armstrong, Glory, and Clint all spoke at the same time.

Mrs. Baldwin raised her brows and looked around the little circle.

Her eyes landed on the boys that still stood against the fence, worried looks on their faces, with the oldest holding the youngest close to him in a brotherly embrace.

Her serious gaze returned to the man holding his ribs. "Armstrong, I know you don't want to hear this, but I really want you to go to the ER. It has to do with our insurance. They will check you out, and if there's nothing wrong, they'll send you right home. In the meantime, Glory will make sure your kids are okay. She's good with children, and kids always enjoy the sale anyway."

"My kids will enjoy the sale, but I don't want to leave without them." His teeth gritted. "I wasn't staying around much longer anyway, because they need to go home and get to bed."

"I'll make sure they get home. I'll make sure they get to bed, and I'll stay until you get back," Glory said. With her mother's blessing, she would take care of this and see it through until the end.

"The two oldest have school in the morning."

"I'll make sure they get on the bus," she said reasonably.

"If I call the ER, and they're waiting on you when we get there, it won't take long. An hour, two, tops. It's a small hospital, and they know how the people around here are. They don't mess around for the sake of messing around." Clint's words were the nail in the coffin, because Armstrong lifted his chin and jerked it a little in assent.

No one had a problem recognizing that for acquiescence, and everyone moved.

Armstrong, his arm still around his upper stomach, his face still pinched tight, walked over to his boys.

Glory's mom moved back as Glory followed him over, taking a deep breath and hoping she didn't look scary to the little kids. Wishing Rose were here. At least until they got used to her.

"This is Miss Glory, and she's going to be taking care of you, probably at least until bedtime. I should be back by morning, okay?"

The oldest nodded. The second tallest boy scrunched his face up, but when he saw his older brother nodding, he did too. The younger two just looked scared.

"I promise I'll be back. Okay?"

At the looks on the boys' faces, Glory's chest pinched. She re-membered that Armstrong's wife had left, and probably the boys worried that he would leave and not come back, too.

It made her sad and also made her determined to do her very best for these little motherless children.

"When you're with me, you get free food, so if you guys like hamburgers and French fries with cheese or ketchup, I've got you covered," Glory said, not sure if that was the best way to talk to kids, but food always made her feel better.

The boys just looked at her, none of them moving to come with her, as Clint checked Armstrong and her mom stood still, giving them time to adjust a little.

"There's also cake, and I know where they hide the candy," she said in a conspiratorial tone.

That made the oldest one smile, although his hand squeezed tighter around his little brother.

"There's candy?" the second oldest said.

"There sure is. What's your name?" she asked, figuring that she probably ought to find their names out before their dad left, since she might not be able to understand them or figure it out herself.

"Benjamin," the little boy said.

That shouldn't be hard. The second child was named Benjamin, second letter in the alphabet. She was terrible with names, always had been, and felt a little pressure, because she really needed to get this right.

"Nice to meet you, Benjamin," she said, holding her hand out.

Benjamin just looked at it for a minute. A cow mooed from somewhere down the aisle, and behind them, a couple of goats baaed.

"Nice to meet you," he said, shaking her hand.

"That's Adam," Armstrong said. "And then you have Caleb and Daniel. Alphabetical." There wasn't any emotion in his voice at all.

She wondered if it was deliberately devoid because of his wife? Or maybe he was just an unemotional person. Maybe that's why his wife had left.

Regardless, she held her hand out to each individual boy. Adam shook it, but Caleb and Daniel just looked at her.

"Let me guess, you guys are four, six, eight, and ten?" she asked, taking a wild guess.

"No. I'm eight," Adam said seriously.

"And I'm six," Benjamin said.

Caleb held up four fingers, and Adam shook Daniel's shoulder, whispering loud enough for everyone to hear, "Tell the lady how old you are."

Daniel stuck a thumb in his mouth and held up three fingers with the other hand.

They were pretty close in age, but Glory's sisters, along with Coleman, her brother, had all been close in age as well.

It made it harder for the parents, which is something she understood as she got older, but much nicer for the kids who had built-in playmates in their family.

"You think everyone's going to be okay if we hit the road now?" Clint spoke loud enough for everyone to hear.

"Yeah. You guys gonna be good?" Armstrong said, his voice holding that same tender tone that he had when he talked to his kids, so different than when he talked to the adults around him.

They nodded stiffly, the anxiety still on their faces, as Armstrong straightened and ruffled the hair of all of them before looking at Clint.

"Let's go." He started walking toward the door, strides that probably would have normally been straight and strong and confident crimped a little from the obvious pain he was in, and his arm still wrapped around his stomach. He leaned forward slightly as well, but otherwise, it was hard to tell that he'd been hurt.

"I'm concerned he might go into shock," her mother said from beside her.

"I've been thinking the same thing. He seems like he's not in much pain at all, but I'm almost positive I heard a crack, although I suppose it could have been a board. I didn't check. I think he's a lot worse off than he's letting on."

"They always are," her mother said, shaking her head.

Her mom had built the auction and livestock business with Glory's dad. When her dad died, she'd taken over, dealing with everything, with Coleman at her side and the girls helping in everything they did.

They didn't stare as the men walked away but turned toward the kids.

"I need to get back to the paperwork if you have these boys?" her mother asked.

"Yeah. We'll be good. I was trying to move that cow out. When she came in, it was just her, but now it's her and her calf, so it's gonna be a little more complicated to get her moving around."

"Yeah. We might have to hold her for a week. I don't think we're going to be able to run them through the arena, and we probably don't want to anyway. I'll check her number and talk to whoever brought her in." Her mom walked over, looking at the tag on the cow's back and pulling out her phone.

Probably to write the information down.

"Have you boys seen a calf before?" Glory asked, assuming that they probably had, since they lived on the farm with Armstrong, but she couldn't remember whether he'd been a crop farmer, or whether he had had pigs or goats or something else.

She just knew she'd seen him before.

"Not one that was just born," Adam said.

"Well, this one was just born in the last hour. Because the mama came in, and it was just her. Now she has a baby."

"Can she break through the fence?" Benjamin said.

"No. These boards are pretty sturdy. But you don't want to put your arm or hand through the fence. Make sure you stay back. Just look through the cracks."

The mom would probably be okay as long as no one tried to get close to her baby, although sometimes cows would get a little crazy when they were penned up. Especially with a little one to protect.

At the very worst, the kids might get their finger smashed if they were holding onto a board, but as long as they didn't stick their head through, they'd be fine.

The boys lined up along the fence, careful to stay back, Adam still holding on to Daniel.

They stood and stared at the cow. She'd licked her calf. He was trying to stand, but she paused and looked at them, her eyes deceptively placid.

"It can't stand up. There's something wrong with it," Caleb said, and those were the first words he'd spoken. For four years old, she thought he talked pretty well, but she hadn't been around a whole lot of children other than helping Rose with her Sunday school class and occasionally teaching junior church.

"It's brand new. It has to learn how to stand up," Glory said, and then she added, "Do you remember when Daniel was born? He couldn't stand up."

"No. I don't remember that." Caleb looked at his brother like the idea that he once upon a time hadn't been able to stand was outrageous.

Daniel had a thumb in his mouth and leaned back against Adam.

They stood and watched the calf for a little bit until it was able to get up. Standing on wobbly legs, it looked so adorably confused that it had been safe and warm just moments ago, and now the coldhearted world intruded.

The boys seemed to get a little restless though, so she asked, "Are you guys hungry?"

She got some nods, so she said, "Can I carry Daniel?"

"Daniel. Let the lady carry you," Adam said, pushing his little brother.

Daniel pushed back against Adam, and Glory grinned. She probably wasn't going to get him to trust her enough to let her carry him around.

"My name's Glory," she said, figuring they might not have heard their dad the first time and they could at least get that so they didn't have to keep calling her "the lady."

"Can I carry you?" She bent down a little to Daniel, deciding she wouldn't know if he'd let her unless she tried.

To her surprise, Daniel took another look at her, sucked on his thumb, and walked the two feet slowly toward her.

She was able to pick him up, grab a hold of Caleb's hand, and herd the rest of the boys out of the aisles.

Whatever they were going to do with that cow and calf, whatever they were going to do with the herd of goats they needed to move, didn't seem to be her concern anymore.

Maybe, if she had time as soon as she got the boys some food, she'd text Lavender and Orchid, her twin sisters, and let them know where she was. But her mom had probably already taken care of it.

These boys were her project tonight; they were worried about their dad and feeling a little lost. She wanted to help them as much as she could.

Pick up your copy of Cowboy Coming Home by Jessie Gussman today!

A Gift from Jessie

View this code through your smart phone camera to be taken to a page where you can download a FREE ebook when you sign up to get updates from Jessie Gussman! Find out why people say, "Jessie's is the only newsletter I open and read" and "You make my day brighter. Love, love, love reading your newsletters. I don't know where you find time to write books. You are so busy living life. A true blessing." and "I know from now on that I can't be drinking my morning coffee while reading your newsletter – I laughed so hard I sprayed it out all over the table!"

Printed in Great Britain
by Amazon

40980112R00099